DAZED & AROUSED

DAZED &
AROUSED

Gavin James Bower

QUARTET

First published in 2009 by
Quartet Books Limited
A member of the Namara Group
27 Goodge Street, London W1T 2LD

A catalogue record for this book
is available from the British Library

ISBN   978 0 7043 7159 0

Typeset by Antony Gray
Printed and bound in Great Britain by
T J International Ltd, Padstow, Cornwall

For N

Acknowledgements

I am hugely indebted to all of those who have read a
draft, or in some cases three, of what is only now,
after their much needed guidance, *Dazed & Aroused*.

I also wish to mention those I approached for help
along the way, especially Niven Govinden, Joe Stretch,
Chris Killen and Stewart Home.

And for allowing me to use a photo that even I can
be happy with, Carl Wilkinson.

My thanks to Annabel Merullo, Tim Binding,
Tom Williams, Claire Daniel and everyone at PFD;
Naim Attallah, David Elliott, Katharine Helmore and
everyone at Quartet – without whom *Dazed & Aroused*
would be in a drawer.

I will always be grateful to my family for supporting
me in pursuing what is essentially
a vainglorious career.

And finally, to Philip Hatfield, Thomas Hudson,
Tristan Thorne, Chris Owen, Carl Davis and,
last but not least, my 'Cool Consultant'
Frances Pollitzer – thank you.

1

Feed Your Addiction is written on the side of a bus advertising a department store and on the surface I can't block out the cacophony of beggars and preachers and shoppers and tourists as they all conspire to confuse and disorientate me.

I'm late. I've arranged to meet my girlfriend for lunch but the casting took longer than expected and I'm rushing through the streets of Soho in a futile attempt to make up for lost time. Sweating from the alacrity of my stride, I dodge a fight between two schoolgirls outside a sex shop on Wardour Street, ignore the admiring glances from butch-looking gay men in Caffè Nero on Old Compton Street and then hurdle an angry delivery boy crouched on the corner of Greek Street, before finally arriving at Soho House.

'You're late,' Nathalie confirms, not looking at me as I approach her table. Nathalie works in PR but looks like a model. She's tall and slim, with blonde, boyish hair, and today is wearing sunglasses even though it's raining outside.

'I know,' I say, sitting down opposite her. 'Um, I'm sorry . . . '

During the silence that inevitably follows, I study her face. Nathalie's skin is pale, her complexion smooth, and the contours of her face – her protruding cheekbones, that angular jawline – are simply breathtaking. She realises I'm looking but still doesn't make eye contact. I lean over to kiss her on the cheek, which is moist, and immediately think to myself that she must've just got here.

'I can't believe it's June!' I say, laughing but not expecting much. 'So . . . how did the interview go?'

'Well, really well,' she answers, nodding assertively and looking down at her nails, which are painted traffic light red.

'Really? That's great. Have you ordered?' I see that she hasn't and am relieved. I take off my jacket, adjust my tie, look around the restaurant. 'Um, do you think you got it?' I ask, trying to attract a waiter's attention.

Nathalie looks at me, her expression earnest, and smiles.

'I'm going to say this only once, Alex, so listen carefully,' she says, reaching across the table and touching my hand. 'For this job, you have to love money.'

2

I'm listening to *This Town* by Frank Sinatra on my iPod on the way to another casting, and the train is in a tunnel, not moving.

This town, is a lonely town . . .

Not the only town, like-a this town . . .

I study my distorted image in the window, playing idly with my hair that looks too long, then grab a *Metro* from behind my seat. The headline reports the execution of a dictator, next to a picture of a reality television star who's lost weight.

This town, is a make you town . . .

Or a break you town, and bring you down town . . .

As I place the paper on the empty seat next to me, a young beggar with rotten teeth enters the carriage and begins asking passengers for help.

'I've gotta survive somehow,' he proclaims to anyone who will listen, holding out a torn McDonald's coffee cup. 'It's better than stealing . . . '

I stare at him, wondering just how young he is.

This town, it's a use you town . . .
An abuse you town, until you're down town . . .

The casting is for Topman and nearly all the boys waiting are teenagers. Most of them just talk about other castings or whether they're going to the shows in Milan, and one boy who's wearing a Kangol hat, like he thinks he's Billy Zane or something, says 'Hey my time is money' to nobody in particular and he's really angry because there are far too many of us here. It's as if agencies across the city have just sent every model without even thinking about it and I end up waiting for over an hour, but they only spend a minute, max, looking at my book.

After I'm done, I wander into a Starbucks and order a latte and tuna melt to go and immediately regret it but can't muster the courage to say anything.

Sitting down by the window as I wait for my sandwich, I begin to absorb the conversations going on at surrounding tables, letting the texture and sensibility of half a dozen simultaneous exchanges wash over me. I isolate one in particular: a discussion between two American men. One man, slim, with a beard and wearing a grey suit and gold jewellery, is talking about a scene in a film during which a teenager plays Beethoven's *Moonlight Sonata* before going on a killing spree.

'What's this supposed to *mean*?' he asks a fidgeting, younger man sitting across from him, before holding up a hand to prevent him from answering. 'It all leads me to ask,' he continues, agitated by now, 'do we actually live our lives, or do we watch others live theirs? Life, as we have come to know it, is played out on television, in movies, on the pages of celebrity magazines. Jesus! Celebrities have become metaphysical entities, brands, commodities, and we all want a piece of it, whether it's real or not. At the same time, poverty, suffering, war, we have come to see as unreal, as somehow removed from us. Explosions over the skies of Baghdad, an African child

11

crying, these are places you and I will never see, people you and I will never meet, and this version of reality is carefully constructed and then represented in between ads for new sofas and shampoo that makes your hair shinier than ever before and YouTube videos of a dog on a skateboard and Paris Hilton sucking someone's cock.' He pauses for a moment, gathering himself. 'Life is a blue screen, my friend, and in that world, you and I, we are not really *here.*'

I look down at my untouched drink.

Careful, the beverage you're about to enjoy is extremely hot.

3

Later that evening, I'm having dinner with Hugo, a friend I've known since university. Hugo's in banking but he keeps changing his job title and, if I'm honest, I don't really know what he does. Tonight, he's come straight from work and is dressed in a new Paul Smith suit, no tie. In front of him, the smallest iPod I've ever seen rests neatly on this month's *GQ.* True to form, he's telling me how I should live my life in between mouthfuls of braised beef shin and a '98 Rioja.

'Let me give you an analogy,' he says sonorously, taking his BlackBerry and a packet of Marlboro Lights out of his jacket pocket and placing them side by side on the table next to his wine glass. 'Remember Oliver from university, the wannabe film-maker?'

I nod, helping myself to one of his cigarettes for later.

'Well, he knows somebody at a production company, some-body who may or may not be able to help him out, who may or may not be able to pass one of his scripts to somebody who counts. That's what it's all about, Alexander. You need to make yourself count.'

As dessert is served – coconut panna cotta for me, crème

brûlée for Hugo – I wonder what it must be like to count, and my thoughts wander to what constitutes a 'proactive initiator', to whether I 'make things happen'.

'I mean, we graduated twelve months ago,' he says. 'What were you doing during your final year? You certainly weren't studying!' Hugo laughs and downs a large gulp of wine. He's quite drunk by now but that doesn't stop him. 'While most people were applying for jobs, what did you do?' he continues gleefully. 'You scraped through your final exams, and now look at you!' He starts to sing *I'm Too Sexy* by Right Said Fred. 'I'm a model and you know what I mean, and I do my little turn on the catwalk . . . yeah on the catwalk . . . ' A pause while he takes another gulp of wine. People are staring at us. 'You've been taken in completely,' he says, now slurring his words, 'by vague assurances . . . by promises of . . . of fame and fortune . . . and all in the name . . . of . . . of beauty . . . and truth!'

A waiter, presumably taking pity on me, interrupts by presenting the bill. As we split it, I spot a man at the other side of the restaurant looking at me, and recognise him instantly. He's a smart-looking, softly spoken black man who asked me out persistently when I worked as a waiter during university. I first met him walking home from work one night. It was late and he was with another man. After making eye contact, he asked for a light and then my name, before enquiring as to the address of the bar. I didn't realise, until he came in the next night and asked me to dine with him at Les Trois Garçons, and then a second time after I told him I had a girlfriend, what he wanted. I've had fantasies of taking him up on his offer, sitting awkwardly in the restaurant, listening to his tiresome attempts at flirtation. We'd end up going back to his place and I'd take a shower. He'd watch as I air-dried in his apartment, desiring my body, lusting after my smooth, muscular buttocks.

Tonight, he's with an effeminate, bitchy-looking blonde

boy, and they're both eyeing me at every chance they get. I soak it up, blanking them as we leave.

There are no cabs and we've missed the last tube, so we make our way back to Hugo's via a passing night bus. Hugo spends the journey talking about his job, but I'm not listening. Instead I watch a feeble-minded man at the front of the bus talking to anybody who'll listen. Really, he's talking *at* them. He says he's going to join the French Foreign Legion and leave this country, because immigrants have taken all the jobs. His lonely eyes are empty.

I eventually look away and out of the window. *Jesus Christ: Worship Him Here* is written on an illuminated notice board in front of a church.

4

I have a shoot today for a four-page editorial in next month's issue of *Wonderworld* or *Wonderland* or something like that and for some reason the call time is 6 a.m. When I arrive at a nightclub in Soho, a little late, a young-looking boy and an older-looking girl are waiting in an empty bar area down–stairs.

'Hi,' I say to the girl, who's very pretty with black hair that's cut in a messy bob and much shorter on one side than the other. 'I'm Alex.'

'Hi,' she says, shaking my hand as I sit down next to her. 'I'm Carla.'

'Hey man,' I say to the boy, who's nervously sipping a takeaway coffee. 'Have you been here long?'

'Hey, yes, I mean, no, not really,' he says. He looks a little scared and doesn't say much for the next half an hour, which is how long we wait before the photographer, a fruity Italian guy, and the stylist, a fruity English guy, arrive.

The photographer, who has a bleached blonde Mohawk, wants us to look 'very natural' so we don't bother with hair and make-up. I put on some loose-fitting jeans that are cropped above the ankle and a pair of purple Dr. Martens and the stylist, who has a shaved head, terrible skin and a bull ring piercing in his huge nose, then proceeds to fuss over whether to put a scarf around my neck but says 'We wouldn't want to cover up that sexy bod' would we?' and decides against it.

I'm up first. I stand on a small stage next to an antique smoking chair, and the photographer keeps saying 'Fabulous!' and 'Gorgeous!' even though all I do is lift my chin and tilt my head to the right, to show my best side, and it doesn't take long before he asks me to change into my second and final look, which is a pair of white briefs, a black PVC waistcoat and the same Dr. Martens.

I sit down by the side of the stage as he shoots the boy, who's wearing an all-in-one vest and shorts outfit and a pair of knee-high socks. He looks like a schoolboy. The photographer asks him to climb onto a small, wobbly-looking table and position himself on all fours. The boy's holding a cigarette and looks awkward but the photographer seems to love it and keeps saying 'Beautiful!' and 'That's it, yes, look vulnerable!' before it's my turn again.

I stand at the back of the stage and the photographer goes for a close-up of me from the waist up, before asking me to sit in the chair with my legs open. He seems to just focus on my crotch but after what feels like no time at all I'm done and as I get changed by the side of the stage the stylist pinches my arse and says 'You were great today!' and I just smile.

On my way out of the club, I watch the boy in his second look. He's only wearing briefs but the photographer has asked him to sit on a rugby ball, which is positioned on the wobbly table. The photographer keeps telling him to pull his briefs down at the back and saying 'More meat!' until all of the boy's hairless arse is revealed, and the rugby ball looks like it's coming out of him or being pushed into him.

5

Hanbury Street in Whitechapel is the scene of the second Jack the Ripper murder and today, on the same street, there's a virtual art installation of two horses in a stable.

I'm wandering around Spitalfields with Andreas, my flatmate, trying to find our next casting. Andreas is with Creative Model Management (like me), has medium to long blonde hair and blue eyes (like me), and is tall and slim with a well-defined body (like me). I assume the agency put us together because they thought we'd have things in common.

Right now, he's trying to talk to me about graffiti but I'm distracted by a beggar ranting indecipherably. *I starve why?* is scrawled on a piece of card in front of him.

'There's more going on there than would appear,' Andreas says in his thick German accent, gesturing at a tag on top of an old pub. 'I mean, for someone to climb all the way up there . . . '

I'm not listening. Instead I watch as a man walks past the beggar and into a sex shop, tripping as he enters.

' . . . they're trying to inscribe a sense of self on a city without self . . . '

Near where we walk, a poster reads: *Fast Getaway Here*.

We eventually find our casting, only to discover that a room full of other good-looking boys and girls beat us to it. As we enter a large reception area, Andreas bumps into someone he knows and, sullenly, I sit down on the floor next to a boy who's reading a book titled *Manufacturing Celebrity*. While I'm still deciding whether or not to pull out my own book, *The Beautiful and Damned*, a boy on the other side of the room whom I've met once or twice spots me and comes over. I think his name is Tobias. He's tall and thin with long white blonde hair tied back in a pony-tail, and he's wearing white skinny jeans tucked into black knee-high boots, a white V-neck T-shirt and a pair of black sunglasses.

'Hey man,' he says, shaking my hand and not taking off his sunglasses.

'Hey,' I reply. 'You been here long?'

'No, not really. But nobody's gone in yet.'

I look at the boy next to me and read over his shoulder.

'We no longer need God because we have celebrities. They have more of everything. More things and more freedom to buy more things . . . '

Tobias asks me something, but I'm not listening.

'What?' I reply, still looking over the boy's shoulder.

'Have you been working much lately?'

'Um, yeah, a little . . . ' I manage, looking back at Tobias. 'You?'

'A little. I got some catalogue work a few weeks ago that paid *really well*. Nothing much else. What do you do when you're not working?'

'What do you mean?' I ask, looking over the boy's shoulder again.

'Jesus fasted to show Man what he could be. Today, we starve ourselves to be like celebrities . . . '

'I mean, do you have another job?' he says.

'Oh, OK. Um, no . . . no, I don't. I've not been doing this for that long and . . . well, um . . . I've been pretty lucky, so far. Why, what do you do?'

'I do 400 metre hurdles,' he says, nodding.

At this point, two male models walk through the door and past us, talking loudly. One of them – young-looking, maybe seventeen, wearing jeans and a fitted white T-shirt – is telling the other about his job.

17

'Yeah, I'm being paid right now,' he says boastfully. 'It's cool. They're really cool about me modelling.'

'That's cool,' the other boy says, staring at him intently.

'Yeah, seven pounds an hour, not bad . . . ' he says, grinning, his eyes widening.

He walks away from the other boy and starts moving around the room, talking to some of the girls.

'Hey girls, do you wanna work at Abercrombie & Fitch? I'm recruiting,' he says to two girls slouching on a sofa in the corner of the room. 'They're really cool about modelling. Most people that work there are models. Here's how it works. You tell them the day before if you have any castings, and they work the rota for the next day around you. I'm working today and am being paid right now. Seven pounds an hour. Not bad . . . '

He only talks to the normal-looking girls, carefully avoiding the weird-looking ones that are here because of their bone structure, because they're 'interesting'. As he moves away after talking to one girl – American-looking, dark blonde, very pretty in a slutty way – she glances at me. We make eye contact and she looks away, only to look back a moment later. I smile and she smiles back, and I consider getting up to sit next to her. As I weigh up the possibilities, I look over the reading boy's shoulder again.

'We buy into this dream to escape our nightmare. But the dream is not real . . . '

Then I realise it's my turn. I leave my bag with Tobias and walk into a small back room, passing a rail of clothing before arriving at a large table behind which four people sit, not looking at me. One of them, a girl, asks me if I'd like to try some jeans on.

'Yeah, sure,' I say, smiling and dropping my trousers.

The jeans are too tight. As I struggle to fasten them, the people behind the table stare at me and the one in the middle – a moody-looking man with blonde hair parted just above his ear and swept across his forehead – looks me up and down, as if considering something very carefully so as to not make a mistake. The girl who wanted me to try the jeans on says 'OK, thanks' before looking at the blonde man and adding 'Unless you want anything else from him . . . ?' which makes me frown involuntarily, but he just shakes his head, still looking at me.

On my way out of the building, I pass the girl from earlier. She's smoking and smiles at me as I stop and pretend to look in my bag for something.

'Hey, I'm Alex,' I say, turning to face her.

'Hey . . . Amanda,' she says, exhaling the smoke to her left. I was right. American.

'Got a light?' I ask, pulling out a cigarette and casually placing it between my lips.

'Sure,' she says, reaching into her pocket and handing me a lighter.

I light my cigarette, look across the street. A bus drives by with an IKEA ad that says *If Your Kitchen Costs Less You Can Work Less* and I turn back to the girl and smile.

'So, how was it for you?' I ask, exhaling to my left and winking.

She laughs, getting my joke.

'That bad?' I say, laughing.

'Yeah . . . I haven't worked in months. My agency told me that I've put on too much weight and I should just eat apples for a while. I need a twenty-two-inch waist, *apparently*. Go and get a fucking fourteen-year-old then . . . ' She sighs, shakes her head, and I laugh, looking down at her waist, which is visible above low cut jeans and looks pretty tiny to me.

'I think you're cute,' I say, smiling again.

'Thanks,' she says, frowning, but in a good way.

I notice she's blushing. 'Hey, I might not know your pain,

but *I* suffer from self-inflicted loneliness and pseudo-depressive angst,' I say, grinning. 'Beat that!'

'You're one too?' she says, smiling. 'I knew it!'

6

I was supposed to be going out with Nathalie and some of her friends tonight, to celebrate her getting the new job, but we had an argument when I told her I'd rather stay in with Andreas and watch television.

There's something on about a new ride at a theme park that simulates a bombing in a crowded urban space. Only an hour ago, on Fashion TV, there was this Italian designer and his new collection, called *Urban Warfare*. Inspired by, in his words, 'terrorist fashion', he'd used material called Ballistic Nylon. Andreas thought this was cool and told me it meant the clothes would be bullet-proof.

We decide to watch a pirate DVD belonging to Andreas, but the audio isn't working. The opening scene is of a man in a bar. He's alone and crying. Nobody around him seems to care.

As Andreas selects the Menu feature on the remote and tries to fix the problem, my thoughts turn to Nathalie. We've been on and off since university but lately things between us have become strained. Little things that shouldn't matter at all have started to irritate me. I've just noticed that she wears too much eyeliner and uses the word 'literally' to emphasise a statement with no figurative alternative. She pretends to be devoid of pretension, but is certain that she is an individual. That she matters.

She doesn't like the modelling either. That's what we fell out about earlier. I told her I didn't want to go out because I have a shoot in Paris tomorrow and an early start, but she wasn't having any of it. What she doesn't understand is that where other people my age have gap years and ski seasons and unpaid internships at ungrateful magazines, I have modelling. You only need to know two things to be a model: how to make looking good look easy, and where your passport is. It pays well, if you get work, and for the very few lucky enough to be the 'right look', it's easy money. Better than a real job, anyway.

I'm not exactly a supermodel – yet – but I've done well so far.

My highlights: a shoot for Paul Smith after I'd only been modelling for two weeks; shows in Milan for Alexander McQueen and Calvin Klein; an exclusive last season in Paris for Yves Saint-Laurent that paid £6,000 and I was flown out for especially; and magazine editorials in more European cities than I care to remember.

There are a few extra benefits too. On top of flights, hotel rooms and cards and prints for my book, my agency pays my rent and gym membership. They even pay when I need a haircut. It just comes off my bill, which I only pay if I work. It's a kind of exclusive credit card that you only pay when you've got more money than you know what to do with.

7

It's 6.30 a.m. and I'm on the Eurostar to Paris trying to get some sleep but the double espresso I had at St. Pancras has just kicked in and the man next to me keeps getting up to go to the bathroom to smoke I assume and so I just look out of the window at passing tower blocks and I notice *Tax The Rich* written on a wall.

I get to Paris earlier than expected and have an hour to kill before I need to be at the shoot so decide to catch the Metro to Châtelet and walk along the Seine and on the platform I see a godly man ranting and wonder what he's so angry about.

The shoot is in Saint-Germain at the photographer's apartment and we're outside for most of the day in the building's communal garden and it's really hot and I'm given a garish shirt and drainpipe jeans and a plastic hood to wear and the photographer keeps saying 'Beautiful!' and 'C'est magnifique!' and the stylist interferes constantly altering a button or moving my hood and a very quiet Japanese man with one half of his head shaved just dusts me with powder every once in a while because I'm sweating from the hood but he's essentially redundant.

We finish early and takeaway pizza appears but I'm not that hungry and need to catch my train home soon so I end up wandering around Saint-Germain for a while and I see two black men butting heads to say 'Hi' in the street and walk past a boutique with a video screen close-up of a man caressing his moccasins and there's a lingering smell of shit on the Metro and it takes a long time to get through security at Gare du Nord and I'm so tired I end up sleeping for most of the journey home.

8

It's Monday but I don't have any castings so, filled with a vague compunction to buy a second-hand book, I catch the tube to Oxford Circus and the bookshops in Soho.

On the tube, a middle-aged woman sitting across from me is talking to her friend.

'Well, there are so many different nationalities you never know, do you?' she says. 'I'm frightened of getting mugged . . . '

At the same time, an older woman next to me is trying to read while shooting glances at the woman opposite. As she reads a copy of *Hello*, looking down her nose at glossy images of celebrities, I study her austere expression. Her lips are pursed and her mouth positioned in such a way as to suggest that she's sucking on something sour. As for the rest of her, well, she's the archetypal middle-class old bag, a gold crucifix proudly displayed within her discreet V-neck sweater and jacket ensemble. Smart-casual.

Walking out of the underground station, transfixed by the ads on the escalators, I almost trip over a beggar colouring in his sign with a felt tip pen. Dazed, I finally reach the surface and make my way through the crowds on Oxford Street, passing two men holding placards. One sells Jesus to passers-by while the other advertises a buffet lunch deal. The former is anxious, even obtrusive; the latter silent and still.

Entering a bookshop on Brewer Street, I realise it's been days since I last talked to Nathalie. I haven't made my mind up *not* to call her but the thought of *not* not calling her is frightening and I honestly don't know what I would say.

As I mull over the possibilities, a young girl reading next to the 'Erotica' section distracts me. She's blonde and petite and is wearing an oversized white dress and a pink beret. I look at her peripherally and can hear her chewing gum. I can even smell it. Drifting closer, I begin to think I recognise her. Her complexion is pale like porcelain, her eyes a startling blue. She looks glossy and new, begging to be touched. I snap out of my reverie as she looks directly at me.

'Hi,' she says, closing a book with a naked girl in a mask on the cover and then moving towards me. 'Weren't you at the Tate the other night?'

'Um . . . yeah, I was,' I answer, surprised by her forwardness and vaguely remembering something about Kandinsky. 'Awful, wasn't it?'

'I liked it!' she replies flirtatiously, hitting me softly on the arm. I spot my chance.

'Yeah well, I guess so, but I find myself dismissing things that don't *move* me.' I say this in an exaggerated way, trying to be funny. 'Anyway, it seemed quite pretentious, whatever it was. Were you there as part of a school trip?'

'I'm not at school, cheeky bastard!' She says this even more flirtatiously and I begin trying to picture her naked, and then naked except for a mask.

'I'm Alex, by the way,' I say, after a moment. 'Pleased to meet you.'

'I'm Emily,' she replies, smiling and shaking my hand.

'Wanna get a coffee?' I ask casually, as if indifferent to her response, which I'm not.

'Yeah . . . OK,' she answers, smiling and clearly keen.

At Oxford Circus, above the steps leading to the underground, I see the scouse preacher who's always there and he looks down on me as we descend into the subterranean depths of the city.

9

The next morning I make my way back home to get changed for a 10 a.m. casting and on the tube I find myself urging the train to go faster while listening to a conversation between two teenage boys. One is tall with long black hair and he's wearing a large black overcoat and sunglasses. The other is smaller, with short hair, and he's wearing exactly the same as the tall boy.

'Self-improvement doesn't interest me,' the tall boy says pretentiously. 'Self-destruction, however . . . '

'But isn't that self-improvement?' the smaller boy replies, after a moment. 'I mean, by your logic . . . '

The tall boy interrupts with a hand gesture, as if stopping traffic, and smiles.

'I count religion but a childish toy,' he says, suddenly making eye contact with me. 'I prefer to play with paradox.'

'Contradiction,' the smaller boy says smugly. 'You mean contradiction, not paradox.'

I feel as if somehow I've heard all of this before and I'm sweating. The train is stopped in a tunnel and hasn't moved in what feels like half an hour. After another moment, the tall boy begins talking again, still looking at me.

'Contradiction is my non-fiction . . . '

At the same time as this, a beggar sitting next to where we stand is reading the *Property Times*.

10

My casting is at a teen magazine on Shaftesbury Avenue. On my way into the building, I see a man with no shoes or socks bending over to pick up something that isn't there and, as I walk past him and through the revolving doors, a couple of security guards surround him slowly and I wonder what will happen next.

There are maybe two dozen other boys standing around on the second floor. As I make my way to the back of what looks like the queue, I study each of them furtively and notice that nobody here looks like me. I sit on the floor and wait my turn.

After waiting for ten, maybe fifteen minutes, I enter a small room with magazine covers of Jennifer Lopez, Beyonce and Jennifer Aniston on the walls. Two women and one man are sitting behind a desk. Both women are thirty-something, blonde and dressed in all black. The man's an old fruit and has grey hair and wears glasses with thick purple frames.

'Hi, my name's Alex, pleased to meet you,' I say, shaking their hands and smiling before sitting down in front of them. I take off my jacket, because it's so hot that I'm sweating.

'So, how long have you been modelling?' asks one of the women, glancing up at me while studying my pictures.

'Not for long . . . um, since I left university last summer . . . ' I open another button of my shirt and roll the sleeves up to cool down.

'So . . . for a year?' says the other woman, staring at me.

'Um, yeah, I guess . . . ' I manage, feeling a little stupid.

'And do you like it?' she asks, flicking quickly through my book. The man's scribbling something on a notepad in front of him but I can't read his handwriting.

'Um . . . yeah, I do,' I answer, trying to sound upbeat. 'It's cool.'

I smile and notice the man is looking out of the window.

On my way out of the building, I see the man from earlier on the street outside. He's sitting on a bench, surrounded by three policemen, and they all look like they're waiting for someone to come or something to happen.

11

I'm in a phone box, thinking about calling Emily. I've spent the whole afternoon looking for my phone. I think I must have lost it somewhere in Paris because I can't find it anywhere, and that's where I had it last.

I decide it's too soon – she'll think I'm needy – so I read the ads promising instant satisfaction instead. One ad, for a tarot hotline, stands out above all others: *HOW WILL I FIND HAPPINESS?*

I call Nathalie and it only rings once before she answers.

'Hey,' she says softly.

'Hey,' I say. 'That was quick . . . '

'What was?'

'Um . . . nothing. So, are you at home? Can I, um, come over?'

'If you want to . . . '

'Well, that kind of depends on you, doesn't it?' I laugh. 'It's your place . . . '

'Only come over if you want to,' she says, interrupting me. A pause.

'Is that a trick question?'

On the tube to Nathalie's, the smell of shit is unbearable. I move carriages in between stops, which helps a little, and there's a young girl – quite pretty, if a little scruffy-looking – sitting across from me drinking a can of Special Brew. I pick up a newspaper that's a day old and am immediately drawn to a front page article on obesity and health drinks. A quote, from the marketing director of Pepsi UK: *With the health and wellness agenda increasing for the consumer, we decided to up-weight our campaign behind Max.*

I smile to myself, look across at the girl, but she's no longer there.

Lying on Nathalie's bed, the television on in the background, I'm cursorily reading the same paper when she gets up and goes to the bathroom without saying a word.

'Alex, can I ask you a question?' she says from the bathroom, after a while. In the paper, I spot an advert for a job as a 'Temporary Trafficker'. 'Have you ever thought about what it would be like to, y'know, be scarred?' she continues, walking back into the room and sitting down next to me on the bed. 'Like, have something really bad happen to your face? Or lose one of your eyes?' Nathalie says this with a look of real anguish, strained, like she's been carrying it around with her for a long time.

'No, not really,' I reply irritably, dropping the paper on the floor by the bed and trying to find something worth watching on television.

'What would you do? I mean, if it did . . . ' she says.

'What would I do? Nothing. What could I do?'

I eventually settle on an episode of an American sitcom I've already seen.

'It scares me a little, y'know? Between you and me, I

27

don't know what I'd do if something like that happened. I have to look away when a bus goes by, or a car skids on a gravelly road, just in case something flies up and slashes my face, or goes into my eye . . . ' She trails off and then frowns, as if realising something. 'Does that make me vain?'

12

I get home to find my dad has called and left a message containing the word 'please' nine times. A demand, so far as he's concerned.

I perfunctorily make myself a sandwich while, on the television, people discuss the War on Terror. A 'Military Analyst' says the people of Iraq are 'ready to embrace modernity' and, for some reason, this makes me recall something my dad once said to me. 'Hitler had some good ideas,' he'd explained. 'Apart from the Jewish thing . . . '

Slouching on the sofa, I turn off the television and open a used copy of *The Picture of Dorian Gray* that I picked up the other day. Inside, I find two bookmarks. The first is a strip of what appears to have been a postcard of a religious image – a young blonde androgynous figure with a crown, sword and halo, like something from a stained glass window. It's addressed to 'Jayne' and says something about coming up over 'Xmas' for a few nights and leaving on Boxing Day. It's dated 19 December 1980, and the postmark is Bethnal Green and Homerton. The card itself was printed in Germany. Stuttgart is mentioned specifically. The second bookmark is a folded personal note, written in slightly different handwriting on paper that's plain on one side and squared on the other, like school graph paper. It's addressed to 'Jane' and reads: *Could you please find a moment for a word with me in the next day or two? Two points, one personal, the other to do with a pupil.*

It's signed with an indecipherable mark, perhaps some-one's initials.

'Jayne', or 'Jane', fascinates me for a moment.

13

I'm in between castings and making my way to Abercrombie & Fitch to buy some T-shirts and shorts because Nathalie's been suggesting we go away together and I'm not sure because I have so many castings but I suppose I could use some new stuff anyway.

As I pass Savile Row I can already detect the almost overpowering smell of cologne and the throbbing beat of teeny-bopper house music and I actually have to queue behind a roped-off area before going in while boys that look like models loiter in the doorway smiling and saying 'Hey how you doing?' as I enter.

I walk past the muscular bloke that stands there all day and into a large building with high ceilings and dim lighting and the music is ridiculously loud and schoolchildren and tourists are pushing past one another scouring the high shelves that you need a ladder to access and fresh-faced boys wearing blue and white pin-striped shirts with the sleeves rolled up and blue jeans and brown flip-flops and skinny young girls wearing blue vest tops and white hot pants and brown sandals are everywhere and standing around doing very little.

I pick up a couple of T-shirts from a large display unit that has maybe a dozen different types of pin-striped shirt before selecting a couple of pairs of shorts from a rack nearby and then I decide against joining the long queue for the changing room because I can always bring them back if they're not right and so make my way to the checkout which has an enormous queue anyway.

Taking my place at the back of the line I spot Amanda standing behind a glass display unit talking to another boy and she sees me looking and I smile and she waits for a moment holding eye contact and then looks away and I think to myself that she doesn't recognise me because it's so dark in here.

14

Leaving Old Street underground station on the way to my next casting, I pull out my new iPhone and see that I have a message and also an e-mail. I bought it to replace the phone I lost and it's handy, I guess, because I no longer need to carry an iPod and a phone at the same time.

I open the message and am disappointed to find I have a casting in an hour, out in Ealing, for a photographer whose name is Bam. The e-mail is from Nathalie. She's just started her new job and likes to tell me how she's getting on, keep me in the loop, y'know, include me in her life. It reads:

Hello my gorgeous model boyfriend,

I got this e-mail today from my boss, who is FAB by the way, and I thought of you. I know you like to be 'in the know' and think you're really cool – but you'll never be as trendy as me! Haha!

Kisses,

Nathalie

p.s. I'm a 'cougar'! Isn't that cool?

Hi all,

Following on from today's presentation by the guys at Cha-Cha, check out the following new terms to use:

• Gastroporn: *turning the mundane chore of cooking into a voyeuristic pleasure, as carried out by celebrity chefs.*

- Cougars: *women, such as actresses Sadie Frost and Demi Moore, whose partners are younger than them.*
- Unilanthropy: *picking a cause and pursuing it strongly in the way Angelina Jolie has done with the plight of orphans.*
- Truth Lite: *political spin and half-truths.*
- Bangalore Envy: *workers' fears that their jobs will be lost as companies relocate to Asia.*
- Adultescents: *young people at a crossroads between living independently and relying on parents (also known as 'Kidults').*
- Churchonomics: *the business of religion as the church in the US grows increasingly commercial.*
- She-E-Os: *female executives that use gadgets like a Black-Berry to manage their personal lives like their careers.*

The guys from Cha-Cha are over from New York for the month and have agreed to come back in and share their wisdom again next week. Let me know if you can attend ASAP – places are strictly limited!

Regards,

Charlotte

15

I'm on my way to meet Hugo at his office while calling Emily to ask if she wants to meet later tonight. It's ringing and ringing and, even though it's been a couple of days and she isn't answering her phone anyway, I still think it's too soon. I think to myself that maybe she's not answering because she doesn't recognise my new number. As I consider this, I step out onto the pedestrian crossing in front of Hugo's office building and a car with a bumper sticker saying *Prepare to Meet Thy God* drives through and almost hits me.

'You're late but I still love you,' says Hugo, getting up from his desk to shake my hand. I didn't realise, until now, that Hugo has his own office with a river view.

'Sorry,' I reply suddenly noticing a girl in the corner behind Hugo's desk, hanging up a large painting of the City skyline. The only colour in the painting is red, for the cranes. 'So . . . where are we going?'

'I want to show you something first,' he answers, visibly excited. He pushes a glossy magazine across the desk. It's a property magazine with a picture of a skyscraper on the cover. The headline boasts: *The Place to Live Above All Others*.

'I'm going to buy a flat in that building,' he announces enthusiastically.

'OK . . . ' I say, not sure what he expects. Hugo, like Nathalie, doesn't really get the modelling thing. He thinks I'm wasting time, procrastinating before I have to commit to a real career.

'I'm not finished,' he adds, grinning inanely. 'I'm going to buy a flat because I've just been promoted!'

I suddenly realise what he wants.

'That's fantastic news, Hugo! Well done . . . '

As I trudge back to my flat later, alone, I see a fight going on down a side street. Two large men are beating up a smaller man, and I start to look away before noticing the smaller man has withered stumps for arms.

Above the scene, on a railway bridge, *We Will Win* is scrawled in red graffiti.

16

I had a casting for a Japanese agency this morning but I've overslept, so rather than turning up late I just don't bother turning up at all.

I take a quick shower and get dressed before wandering into the kitchen and then realising I have nothing in. I'm starving, though, so decide to go out and pick up bread and tea bags. While looking for my shoes in the lounge, I notice I have a new message from my dad and I start it but don't get to the end.

It's really bright outside and also hot and across the road from Tesco Express I see a drunk staggering along the pavement, leering forwards and barely able to stay on his feet. It's not yet noon. As he passes, I notice that he's shat himself, the stain visible on the seat of his blue jeans. He falls down in a heap. People ignore him.

I go back to my flat and spend most of the day watching the twenty-four-hour news channels repeat the headlines. In the afternoon, there's a kind of debate about condoms, and a religious leader argues vehemently that abstinence is the best form of contraception. I wonder to myself, as he argues this, would he fuck God?

Later, I steal a bus journey to Nathalie's and sit at the back staring at the television screen. Some have CCTV but this one has advertising and celebrity news. It doesn't have sound, though, presumably because that's too invasive.

As I look out of the window at passing cars, I spot one with a bumper sticker that says *I'm going to Heaven, wanna come?* and I watch as the car overtakes us, wondering how they're so certain.

I look around the bus. Nobody is talking.

17

'When I'm not with him, for like, *a day*, it feels like forever . . . '

I've finally got hold of Emily, only to have to put up with her droning on about how much she loves her boyfriend. It's 9 a.m. and I'm on my way to a very early go-see, walking through a subway somewhere in Dalston, struggling to balance my phone in between my ear and shoulder as I re-read the call sheet. *DON'T SUBMIT TO DE-HUMANISATION* is written in large letters on the wall, next to where a beggar tries to sleep.

'That's great, Emily, really great,' I say.

'What?' she yells. 'Your signal's gone and I can't hear you, Alex. Speak up!'

'Whatever,' I mutter, and hang up.

I give up on the go-see and decide to go to my next casting instead. It's a request for a well-paid look book job and I need to be there by 10 a.m., so it's the right decision.

I catch a bus to Highbury & Islington before jumping on the tube to Oxford Circus. On the train, a red sticker saying *Destroy Advertising* is stuck on an empty ad bracket above my head.

I get to Oxford Circus in no time at all, despite the time of day. As I push my way down Oxford Street and look at the call sheet to confirm where the casting is, an old man wearing a white T-shirt, torn jogging bottoms and a baseball hat overtakes me. On the back of the T-shirt, almost illegible in black marker pen, it says *Tony Blair and MI5 tried to MURDER me.* He's ranting to himself in a thick cockney drawl but I can't make out what he's saying. As I get closer, trying to understand him, the old man stops at a rubbish bin in front of McDonald's and sifts through it, still talking to himself, and I pass him and make my escape down Ramillies Street.

18

'When you watch TV, do you know why the adverts are louder than the film you're watching?' asks Nathalie, stubbing out a cigarette as a waiter clears our empty coffee cups.

'Go on,' I answer, feigning interest. I'm in between castings and Nathalie and I are having lunch in a café near her work. It's really hot again today, so we're eating outside.

'Two reasons. First, they shock you out of your stupor. Second, they keep your attention when you're out of the room, making a cup of tea or whatever. Whether you like it or not, Alex, that's clever.'

My phone rings before I can even contemplate a reply. It's an unknown number, but when I answer I'm greeted by the voice of my dad.

'Ah, hello at last!' he says.

'Hello,' I reply, excusing myself and walking away from our table, out of earshot.

'I've been trying to reach you for a week now, Alexander,' he says, clearly annoyed but trying to cover it with laughter. 'Why don't you answer your phone?'

'I've been . . . um . . . busy . . . sorry,' I manage.

'How are you enjoying my membership to Soho House? I see last month's bill was an all time record . . . '

'Um, yeah . . . sorry about that . . . '

'I want to meet up,' he interrupts. 'Is that OK with you?'

'Sure,' I say flatly, after a moment.

'Well, I'll be in London tomorrow so let's have dinner. I'm staying at the Ritz so how about we eat there?'

'What time?'

'I'll call tomorrow to confirm . . . '

'You don't need to,' I say, interrupting him. 'Just give me a time and I'll be there.'

'OK . . . how about, 9.30?'

'Fine. See you then.'

'Great, just great. I'll look forward to it. I . . . I miss you, son.'

A pause.

'See you tomorrow,' I say, and hang up.

19

Condoms in the 'Family Planning' section in Boots; a sign saying *Where Older People Can Find Care In Housing* outside an old people's home near a casting the other day; a fridge magnet belonging to Nathalie that says *Born Free, Now Expensive* . . .

I'm running late to meet my dad for dinner, daydreaming in the back of a cab. When I finally arrive at the restaurant, after walking from Piccadilly Circus because the cabbie was useless, my dad's already at a table drinking champagne with Catherine.

'Sorry I'm late but . . . I had a casting,' I explain, sitting down. 'Have you ordered?'

'No we haven't,' my dad answers, clearly annoyed. 'We knew you'd make us wait, so it's not a problem. You're here now. That's all that matters.'

Catherine, who's wearing a revealing black dress, so revealing I can see her implants, has her arm in his and is laughing. She does the weather on television, even though she has a lisp, but she's OK I guess. Apart from being a home-wrecking whore, that is. I nearly shout this out but instead just smile.

'Hi Catherine, how are you?' I say.

'I am very well, thank you,' she answers. 'You look very hand*th*ome tonight, Alexander.'

My dad laughs, almost choking on his champagne.

'Yes. My son, the supermodel! I'm very proud!'

People are looking at us and I want to disappear but instead I simply ask a waiter for another glass. He brings one almost immediately and fills it with Dom Pèrignon '96.

'Thanks,' I say, before downing it.

'What wa*th* it for?' Catherine asks.

'Sorry?' I say, confused.

'The casting that made you late,' my dad adds, staring at me.

'Oh, the casting!' I manage, realising how hollow this sounds. 'Um . . . Dior. It was for Dior . . . '

'I bet that pay*th* well!' Catherine says.

'Not as well as a real job!' my dad interjects, laughing again.

'How long are you in town for, Dad?' I ask, changing the subject.

'I'm here for the weekend. I have an important lunchmeet with some clients on Monday, but then we're off to New York, aren't we darling?' He kisses Catherine on the ear and she giggles and I want to be anywhere but here and so I look away, around the restaurant. The room is full of old men with younger women and I realise that I'm the youngest person here and start to wonder whether anyone else has noticed this.

When dinner is over and we're outside waiting for my cab, my dad hugs me and slips me £250 in cash.

'Thank you for seeing me, son,' he says, holding me tighter.

'That's fine,' I say, standing on my tiptoes awkwardly, as if I've been turned to stone. I don't tell him what I really think, that I'm disappointed in him and feel let down, and I also don't tell him that when Catherine says goodbye she whispers in my ear and says 'You're gorgeous' and squeezes my arse while he talks to a doorman.

I wouldn't want to disappoint him.

20

Jo, my booker at my agency, thinks it's a good idea for me to have a haircut. 'Nothing drastic,' she'd told me on the phone earlier. 'Just a change.' I've been growing my hair for a while but am open to suggestions, so I go to a new salon she tells me is 'very *now*!' on Cheshire Street, in Shoreditch.

There are only models in the salon and all the hairdressers are male. I'm reading the Proust Questionnaire in *Vanity Fair* when an oldish lady comes to the door but is reluctant to enter. Her face is very red and she looks drunk but reasonably affable, with a screwed-up newspaper stuffed down her oversized overcoat. The man who's cutting my hair sighs and walks over to the door to talk to her and I listen in.

'I'm a Tibetan monk? In my soul? *Yeah* . . . ?' she says, the intonation suggesting every sentence is a question.

It transpires that she wants a wet shave but the hairdresser tells her he can't take it that close and they discuss this for a moment but neither is willing to budge.

I look beyond them and out of the salon. On the other side of the street, *POWER TO THE PEOPLE UNTIL ALL ARE FREE* is written in black on the wall of a derelict building.

After I'm done, I make my way up Brick Lane to Bethnal Green Road to catch a bus home. My phone rings. It's Jo.

'Hi babes,' she says. 'How did the salon go? You looking gorgeous?'

'As ever . . . ' I say. 'Yeah, it looks fine,' I add, after there's no reaction. I walk past a block of ex-council flats and there's a poster saying *They're Only After Your Money* in a window on the top floor.

'Come by later and show us, OK?' she says. I think I hear

someone giggling in the background, probably Sam, one of the other bookers.

'OK, but . . . '

'Babes,' she interrupts, 'I know I told you earlier you didn't have any castings but . . . you've got one right now. It's at *Dazed & Confused* and . . . '

'Alex?' I hear someone interrupt. Sam has joined the call.

'Hi Sam,' I say.

'Look babes, it's really just a go-see but they're planning a shoot with Kate and Rankin soon and they really like your look and it's going to be big so definitely worth checking out. It's nearby anyway . . . '

'OK, Alex?' says Jo, after a moment.

'No problem.'

I walk back along Bethnal Green Road and make my way into Hoxton, wandering under the subway at the roundabout on Old Street, avoiding groups of school kids and fashionistas and beggars and taking in the smell of kebab houses and traffic as I move closer to *Dazed & Confused*. Looking up, counting the numbers on the doors, I see *Regime Change Begins at Home* scrawled in red spray paint above a laundrette. Below this, *Inaction is a Weapon of Mass Destruction* is written in large black letters.

I eventually find the right building and walk into a small entrance room, but nobody's around. There's a table and chair at the back and a coffee table in the middle with piles of the latest issue on it, and next to the table is a huge board with an old cover of a topless Kate Moss, photographed by Rankin. Out of nowhere, a girl appears.

'Hi-ya, you 'ear for the car-stin' darlin'?' she says in a Lily Allen-esque accent. 'Oh my days it's hot today innit?'

'Yeah,' I answer. 'I mean, yes, I'm here for the casting . . . '

'Folla me then darlin'.' She leads me through a passage-way to a large door, types in a code and stands aside.

'Thanks,' I mutter, smiling as I enter.

Inside is another reception room with more magazines and another giant board, this time with Carl Barat on it. Sitting side by side on a large leather sofa are three girls and facing them on a chair is an American-looking boy with muscular arms.

I stand close by and am about to lean against the board with the giant face on it when I realise what I'm doing and move away to a safer standing place by the opposite wall. My palms are sweating and I wipe them on my jeans because I don't want to shake hands with sweaty palms. From where I'm standing, I can see groups of people moving around, sitting at desks doing various things, and they all look young and quite cool but also grubby. I spot a young girl working over by the opposite side of the room who looks like Emily from the back and I will her to look at me and make eye contact, but before she can the boy walks past me and I realise it's my turn.

I walk over to the girls, all of whom look pretty similar – in their twenties, kind of cool, not pretty – and shake their hands, introducing myself.

'Hi, I'm Alex, pleased to meet you,' I say, smiling.

'Hi, thanks for coming in,' the girl on the left says. The girl in the middle alternates between looking through my book and staring at me, while the girl on the right looks over her shoulder.

'So, how long have you been modelling?' asks the one on the right.

'Um, just since university,' I answer.

'Are you free on Friday?' asks the one on the left. 'That's when we'll be shooting.'

The girl in the middle takes three cards without saying a word, which I think is a good sign.

'Um, yeah, I think so,' I say, trying to think and then realising I need to sound keen, 'Um, yes, I'm free.'

As I get up to leave, a man who looks a lot like Jefferson Hack walks past. He's wearing high-top trainers, skinny jeans and a T-shirt with the sleeves rolled up, and there's a pack of cigarettes concealed under the right one. His hair is shaved short at the back, sides and on top, but for some reason the fringe has been kept long. I follow him out of the building and as he stops to light a cigarette we make eye contact, and I decide it is Jefferson Hack and smile, wondering to myself what Kate Moss ever saw in him.

21

I can't sleep that night because I'm so excited and by 6 a.m. I find myself just staring at the television, watching the breakfast news. Politicians are beamed into the room but their rhetoric is lost on me because the television's on mute. All I can do is look at various suit and tie combinations, and think of the word 'immaculate'.

Later, on the way out of my flat to go to a shoot, I suddenly remember the television's still on. As I go back to turn it off, an ad grabs my attention, and an authoritative voice assures me that superficial change is good and we have nothing to fear, as corner shops become corner boutiques become corner showrooms become corner restaurants . . .

Zurich: Because Change Happenz

22

I've just left the shoot and it was for a new hair gel that's hood resistant and I'm now running late for dinner with Nathalie and her new work friends and it starts raining as I cross Wardour Street on my way to a new sushi bar that's just opened next to a new Starbucks I think when I bump into a very pretty girl I met once doing something somewhere that escapes me for a moment but I instantly remember as she yells 'Oh my God Alex!' at the top of her lungs.

'Oh hi Frankie' I say and then realising I need to sound enthusiastic desperately add 'God you look great how long has it been six months?'

'No babes' she says seductively 'we saw each other last week don't you remember?'

'Oh yeah' I say hitting my head with the palm of my hand and then lowering my voice add 'how could I forget?'

'I should hope you couldn't!' she says and laughs as if remembering something but not wanting to tell me what it is 'I just saw you in *Wonderland* and I almost died so you have to come to mine tonight because I'm having what will be the best party!'

I tend to stretch out goodbyes with near strangers but suffocated I eventually break free by saying I will and as I run through Soho skilfully dodging Japanese tourists and *Big Issue* sellers I see a young beggar with rotten teeth staring at me smiling and saying something I'm unable to fully catch.

On Dean Street I can hear music from bars the visceral sounds of people out with friends and I can't get the smiling beggar out of my mind.

I notice the rain has cleared, and everything slows down.

I stop walking, and stare at my reflection in the filthy window of a derelict shop.

Studying my smeared image, I begin to smile, and mouth the words 'We . . . will . . . win'.

23

The party takes place on a Range Rover-lined street in the heart of Chelsea. Her mum and dad are divorced but the former cashed in big time as a result, so this huge town house now belongs to Frankie.

I arrive at midnight but there aren't that many people here and it feels like it's barely started. The DJ, a pretty teenage boy wearing black Wayfarer sunglasses, starts playing *Song for Clay (Disappear Here)* by Bloc Party as I walk through a large hallway and upstairs, squeezing past incredibly pretty teenage girls who all look like models. On the landing, there's a huge montage made up of old covers of *The Face*. Beautiful faces are everywhere. After standing in front of it for a moment, I make my way into a large kitchen, helping myself to a glass of punch from a huge bowl on a dining table that's been set for a dozen people. I look out of the window at a group of rich boys gathering in the garden. They all look younger than me and I think a few of them maybe work at Abercrombie & Fitch. As I turn around to leave the room, Frankie appears, taking me by surprise.

'Hi Alex!' she shrieks, kissing me on both cheeks. 'So glad you came!'

'Hi . . . again,' I say, looking her up and down as discreetly as possible. She looks thin, but in a good way, and is wearing a white crinkled vest dress, possibly Kate Moss Topshop. 'How are you?'

'My nose hurts,' she answers, placing her hands on my waist as she moves past to pour herself a drink.

'Yeah?' I ask, taking the opportunity to admire her from behind through the diaphanous dress.

'It hurts because I put too many drugs up it.'

We're interrupted when a girl enters the room, speaking

loudly on her phone. She's wearing a fitted basketball vest, tiny hot pants and Ugg boots. As she rests the phone on her shoulder and fills two glasses with punch, we both stare at her, listening in.

'Yeah I know, he was so drunk he pissed himself in his sleep,' she says, not laughing.

24

'I need a cigarette,' I say to Frankie, toying with my lighter as we lie next to one another on her bed. Realising she's asleep, I get up and begin navigating my way through the house. It's 4 a.m. but *Blue Monday* by New Order is coming from a room downstairs and most people are still here, some dancing, some just sitting around, watching television and smoking joints.

Frankie's a part-time fashion student and part-time model. I met her during London Fashion Week. She was casting men for a show at her college, and she booked me so she could meet me again. That's what she told me, anyway. Frankie's only 5' 5", too short to be a catwalk model, but her feline features and amazing body more than make up for it and she gets a lot of work. She gets what she wants in other ways too. It's just the way she is. She can have any boy she wants, and I've never known her to not be seeing at least a couple at any one given time. The day we met, she told me she'd like to be an actress and had started taking lessons. I told her I thought she'd probably be good at it.

On the terrace outside, the party behind me, I listen to the sounds of the night. It's still warm and I light a cigarette, letting the flat sensation that exists when life is momentarily blocked out wash over me.

25

I wake up in Frankie's bed, alone. It's light, but I don't have any way of knowing what time it is. As I get up and begin looking for my phone, the bedroom door opens. It's Frankie.

'Looking for this?' she says, teasing me from the doorway, my phone in her hand. She's wearing a towel and I just stand there for a moment, in front of a large walk-in closet that's the size of my bedroom, not sure what to do.

'It's afternoon, sleepy head,' she says, smiling and walking towards me.

'Really? I had no idea . . . '

'Are you hungry?' she interrupts, brushing past me and standing in front of the closet, not going in.

'Um, yeah . . . yeah, I am actually,' I manage, sitting down on the edge of the bed, for some reason nervous.

'They're making a fry up downstairs, but I don't think it's ready yet . . . '

In the mirror by the door, I watch as Frankie drops her towel on the floor, moves slowly towards the closet and disappears inside.

26

I'm on my way to meet Hugo for a drink. On the tube, I find myself staring at an overweight man opposite me. He bulges through his shirt buttons and takes up close to two seats. His kind yet simple-looking face appears strained and is enveloped by a mass of fat that should be his neck and chin.

I get off at Embankment and walk across the bridge, passing a beggar on his knees.

When I finally reach the bar, half an hour late, I spot Hugo on the terrace. He's sitting at a table and talking to a girl I don't recognise.

'Hi,' I say. 'Sorry I'm late but I . . . '

'No need to apologise, my friend,' he says, standing up to hug me. He pulls me close and kisses me hard on the cheek. 'Good to see you buddy. You know Lisa . . . '

'Um . . . hi,' I say, turning to face her.

'Hi Alex,' she says with utter indifference. She's smoking and exhales to her right before extending her hand.

'Likewise,' I say, shaking her hand quickly and sitting down. She's not pretty enough to be so cold, I think to myself as I attract the attention of a passing waitress. 'Can I get a beer?'

'So Lisa, young Alexander here is having a spot of woman trouble,' says Hugo, smiling. 'Isn't that right my friend?'

'Um, well . . . ' I start to say, before trailing off.

'Now now, don't be shy,' he says. 'Shall I explain? OK, so Alexander has a girlfriend – the lovely Nathalie – and he's also just started seeing a hot little number called Francesca. *Again*.' He laughs. 'Now, that would be enough for most people but not our Alexander. Oh no! He's also trying to find his way into the panties of another girl, a schoolgirl called Emily. Is that right my friend, or have I somehow failed to convey the intricacies of your infidelity?'

Lisa giggles hysterically and I can't bear another minute.

'I need to take a piss,' I say.

'Charming,' says Hugo, not looking at me as I get up from the table.

In the toilets, I see I have a text from Nathalie asking me to meet her later tonight and I consider this for a moment in the safe confines of a cubicle, before noticing *Art is dead do not consume it's corpse* is written on the back of the door in large red letters.

I sit down on the toilet seat, unable to take my eyes off the out-of-place apostrophe.

27

I spend most of the next day lazing around at Frankie's. At some point in the afternoon, while I'm in one of Frankie's three living rooms watching *Donnie Darko*, Sam calls asking me to meet a photographer across town. As I desperately think of an excuse not to go, Frankie enters the room and presents me with a cup of tea. I smile as she sets it down on the coffee table, before climbing over me on the sofa, kissing me on the cheek and reclining with her bare legs on my lap.

'Um, I'm in the middle of something actually,' I manage. 'Not sure I can make it in time and, um, I haven't even got my book . . . ' This is a lie. I am never without my book.

'Look, it's in South East London, so you can come by the agency and pick up ours,' she says. 'As long as you bring it back today.'

I look at the television screen. American teenagers are walking through the corridors of a high school and everything's in slow motion. In the playground, some young girls dressed in school uniforms start dancing to *Head Over Heels* by Tears For Fears and at that exact moment Frankie begins tickling me and giggling hysterically.

'Yeah . . . um . . . ' I say, squirming on the sofa, 'but I'm not sure I can . . . get there in time . . . '

'You've got over an hour – no Jo, Marcus can't do then because he's in Milan – Alex, you still there? See you soon babes.' She hangs up.

28

My agency is in the heart of Soho on Poland Street. The buzzer doesn't work but the front door is always open, and the men's division is on the fourth floor but the building has no lift.

I walk into the reception area and see a couple of male models I don't recognise waiting, drinking water from blue plastic cups and flicking through fashion magazines that are piled neatly on a coffee table. I smile at the receptionist – a temp, young, quite cute, bad skin – and nod at the models. They both look American, are wearing shorts and sandals and have the same haircut – shaved short at the back and sides, heavy through the fringe – but one of them looks more worked-out than the other.

'Hey man, how you been?' the buff one asks as I walk past, standing to shake my hand.

'Hey,' I reply, turning back to face him.

'Did you get that job?' he says, whispering. 'You know, Kate Moss. I saw you there . . . '

'Um, I don't know actually,' I say, looking over my shoulder in case someone's behind me and then, lowering my voice, 'why, did you?'

'I didn't hear anything. The money's shit anyway . . . '

I look behind him at the other boy. He appears to be lost in a magazine and is just staring at an ad for handbags. Four beautiful and tan young girls are staring back with such intensity that they seem somehow to be looking beyond the lens.

'I've got to see Jo anyway,' I say, after a moment. 'Catch you later.'

'Are you going to fucking Milan?' he half asks half groans.

'Probably . . . I guess . . . ' I say, turning and making my escape.

I walk into the main room of the agency, which is painted garish purple and gold and full of weird furniture – a chaise longue that nobody's allowed to go near, an enormous furry cube, a transparent plastic table with matching chairs – but the bookers are oblivious to it all and on the phone, transfixed in front of old PCs, as if they work in a call centre.

'Hi babes,' says Jo, getting up from her seat and kissing me on both cheeks. Jo's in her thirties and has very short bleached blonde hair and smokes, a lot. 'You look tired.'

'Um, yeah, I am . . . are you OK?' I say as her phone rings.

'Yeah babes. Just busy busy busy, you know how it is. Can I talk to you after this call?' she says, already putting her headset on.

I walk through the main room to the kitchen and help myself to a glass of water. In a room across the hall, I can hear a conversation going on between Guy, who owns the agency, and a skinny young girl with long red hair and freckles.

'We love your look, babes,' he tells her, gushing. 'You're like a younger, prettier Nicole Kidman. Has anyone ever told you that? You're very *now*!'

'Thank you,' she says, letting out a giggle, 'but do you, um, think I can earn a lot of money?'

'Look, you could earn ten grand or you could earn a hundred grand. We don't make promises, but I've been doing this for the last fifteen years and I'm not in the business of being wrong. You're going to be big, I promise you.'

I go back to men's division and sit down next to Jo, who's now off the phone.

'So, did you make your casting this morning?' she asks.

'What casting?' I ask, genuinely clueless.

'I sent you a text last night,' Sam interrupts. Sam's younger than Jo and used to be a model, but she's not attractive at all and is a real bitch.

49

'I didn't get it, I guess,' I manage. 'Um, I'm sorry . . . '

'This is why you need to check in, babes,' says Sam condescendingly. 'Every day between 5 and 6.'

'Sorry. Sure. I, um, forgot . . . '

'OK, so here's our book,' says Sam, handing me a portfolio. 'You have to promise me you'll bring it back straight after your go-see, OK?' Her tone is deadly serious but she's smiling and touching my arm. I nod. 'Your agency in Milan called and they would like you to stay on after the shows,' she continues, sitting back down and not looking at me. 'They wanted you to do that last time, remember? We'll see, though, because there's loads going on here and you'll probably get work in Paris – and you can always go out to Milan in the autumn.' Jo stands up and nods as Sam says this last part, as if they've both planned it already anyway.

'Fine,' I say, standing to leave. 'When am I flying out for the shows?'

'Sunday – Paris first, then Milan for castings and shows,' says Jo, skipping out of the room. 'And then back to Paris,' she adds, loudly.

'OK,' I say, walking over to the door. 'Um, I guess I'll see you later . . . '

'Don't forget the book!' Jo shouts, by now invisible. 'And get some sleep!'

29

An hour later, after changing to an overground train at London Bridge, I get to my go-see in Woolwich Arsenal. As I leave the station and pull out my street map, I realise everyone is black and wonder if I should notice this but can't help it.

I look at my call sheet. Leo, the photographer, lives in an apartment building over by the river. I follow the map as I cross a busy main road, leaving behind a depressing street market of shabby-looking stalls selling faux-designer clothing and pirate DVDs.

I eventually arrive at a large housing complex of modern-looking apartments – the kind of thing young professionals who can't afford somewhere central choose to live in. It's on the site of what used to be the Royal Arsenal and the developers have incorporated most of the outer structure and many of its features into the design. There's a sign explaining the history of the site and how the new site 'preserves the tremendous and vital heritage of the area'. Standing within the complex, looking for the right building, I think of the word 'exclusive' and wonder to myself whether this is what a ghetto feels like, but I can't see any armed guards with dogs, just one small fat bloke in a booth, dressed like a parking attendant.

When I do find the right building, I realise I need a code but some people let me in inadvertently by neglecting to close the gate behind them. I knock on the door of 123a, wait for a moment, and just as I'm about to knock again the door swings open and a very handsome blonde boy appears.

'Hey man – in there,' he says, gesturing behind him and brushing past me, as if in a hurry.

The apartment feels large and is split into two levels. On the ground floor, there's a long corridor with a bathroom on the left and stairs on the right, and then one large open-plan living space at the end. I walk through into the living room where a man is standing with his back to me. He's wearing a purple trucker hat, a gold oversized string vest, grey jogging shorts and a pair of white Reebok Pump trainers. I can see that he's got a beard and from the side is quite good-looking, if a little overweight.

'Hi . . . ' I venture.

'Oh hi, sorry, I didn't see you there,' he replies, looking me up and down. 'I'm Leo. Come in and have a seat.'

'I'm Alex, pleased to meet you,' I say, shaking his hand and sitting down as instructed. I start to get out my book.

'No no, you won't be needing that,' he says, a little agitated. He smiles and adjusts his hat, strokes his beard. 'I'll just take some Polaroids. I have something for you to, um, try on.' He comes over to me carrying two glasses of water, sets one down next to me and walks over to a chair on the opposite side of the room. 'How long have you been modelling?' he asks, after a moment.

'Not long,' I answer quietly, then speaking up, 'just since university.' I take a gulp of water. Looking at him, sprawled across his seat, I notice that his shorts are ridiculously tight and leave nothing to the imagination.

'Cool . . . that's cool . . . ' he replies, staring at me for a moment and then smiling. 'OK, so I'd like you to try one or two things on. Upstairs on your right is a room with some clothes and to your left is where I'll shoot you. Help yourself to an outfit and I'll see you up there.' At this point, I realise there are other people in the flat because there are noises coming from upstairs.

I smile, say 'Sure' and then make my way out of the room, leaving him with my book just in case and immediately afterwards remembering I don't have any cards with me.

After making my way upstairs I take a right and for some reason knock on the door as I enter. Inside what looks like a bedroom are three male models, all changing back into their normal clothes. I notice one is naked and standing awkwardly, facing the other way so I can just see his hairless arse and balls hanging down in between smooth muscular legs. I look away and at a rack of clothes on the other side of the room, and am confronted by what I'll have to wear. The choice is a pair of transparent PVC trousers and matching vest, or a pair of white Y-front briefs. I opt for the latter, not second-guessing my decision for a moment.

By the time I've undressed and put on the briefs, the other boys have gone. I make my way tentatively across the hall to the other room, where I can hear Leo setting up. I enter a completely empty room with floor-to-ceiling windows obscured partially by a large white board, upon which are pinned Polaroids of male models wearing very little. I notice he's taken off his vest.

'It's so hot isn't it?' he says, playing with the camera. 'OK, I just need a few shots of you in this outfit.'

I stand and pose and go through the motions. Lift my chin, tilt my head to the right, put my chin down, look straight ahead. Clench my jaw, unclench. I lean on the wall behind me with my hands behind my back or stand upright with my arms by my side. Leo keeps saying 'Beautiful' and 'Yeah that's it' and 'That's great' and even one 'Hot! Very hot!' before suddenly stopping.

'OK,' he says, 'put your hands in your pants and pull them down a little so I can see your pubes.' I do as he says. 'A little lower . . . ' he continues and then, when I do as he asks, adds, 'even lower . . . great, that's great.' The base of my penis is now visible and he keeps shooting me and when he tells me to grab my balls, hard, I do and he shoots some more. 'OK, that's enough,' he says, putting the camera on a table in the far corner of the room that I didn't see before.

'Cool,' I say, on my way out of the room.

'No wait!' he says, almost panicking. 'I need one more shot,' he continues, calmer now. 'It's a full length shot but I, um, need to see you naked because the shoot is going to involve nudity.' I must look surprised because he adds, 'I told your agency and they said it was cool . . . '

I take off the briefs and walk back to where I was before, while absent-mindedly adjusting my genitals.

'Here?' I gesture, pointing to the wall. I look down and see that my penis is slightly aroused. In a good way.

'Yeah . . . that's great . . . ' he says, already shooting me.
I look over at the white board and try to see if there are any
nudes. I can't see any. ' . . . that's just perfect . . . '

30

I leave the go-see and notice I have a missed call from my
agency. As I wait for the train back into London, I give them a
call.

'It's Alex,' I say. 'You called?'

'Great news babes!' says Sam excitedly. 'They love you at
Dazed and want you for the Kate Moss shoot. It's tomorrow.
I'll send you the details.'

'Um . . . wow, that's great,' I say. 'Is it, um . . . is the
money any good?'

'No not at all. But you're going to be in an editorial with
Kate-fucking-Moss, so get excited babes!' She laughs. 'Call me
if you don't get the details and then tomorrow after you're
done. We want to know how it goes!' She hangs up.

On the train, I pick up a free newspaper and begin reading
something on an art gallery that exhibited a wooden plinth,
despite it actually being the base for a missing sculpture.

'What is art?' the reporter asks in the penultimate para-
graph. Rhetorically, I guess. Well, according to the gallery,
unwilling to accept the mistake, the plinth is. The sculpted
head was 'judged separately' and ultimately 'rejected'.

31

I'm sitting on a bench waiting for a train to go to my shoot and I'm running late and need to catch an overground train at Liverpool Street and I didn't sleep at all last night so am not really in the mood for this.

The man sitting next to me on the bench gets up and starts wandering down the platform, so I pick up the newspaper he left behind. The headline on the front-page says *SHORTS BAN IN HEAT WAVE* and I look up and watch as a train pulls up on the westbound platform, across from where I'm sitting. I notice that more and more people are gathering on the platform next to me, waiting anxiously, looking up at the screen, which gives no indication as to the whereabouts of the next train.

I put the newspaper down on the bench to my right and when I look to my left I spot the old man from Oxford Street walking down the platform. On the front of his T-shirt, written in black marker, it says *Tube prices 5 x NYC = BLIAR!* and he's talking loudly to himself, something about the tube prices and he keeps saying 'Tony Blair!' and 'Mr Blair!' at the end of his sentences, the intonation on the last syllable as if to emphasise his point. He's handing out bits of paper and when he passes I extend my hand and he gives me one page of a Transport for London information brochure that's been dismantled. His T-shirt message is written on the page in black marker. As he makes his way back up the platform, we make eye contact and he comes to sit next to me.

'I'm not a Communist, I'm not a Red,' he says to me, face unshaven, his expression determined. 'Filthy they is. They wanna see England go to the dogs. I love this country . . . I'm an Englishman!'

I want to tell him that Tony Blair is no longer Prime Minister, but before I can he gets up and walks away. As he makes his way up the platform, he turns around and shouts 'Mr Blair!' and then disappears.

32

I'm staring out of the window at the City View Hotel in Hackney, which looks out onto the train track that I'm now crawling along, making me even later for my shoot.

After eventually getting to Hackney Downs, I spend ten minutes walking around in blazing heat trying to find the right address. When I finally arrive, I'm buzzed in by a girl. I navigate my way around old bikes in the hall and corridor, through what looks like an unused building to a back staircase, which leads to a green door on the building's top floor. A young girl, presumably the one that buzzed me in, opens the door just before I knock.

'Um, hi,' I say. 'I'm . . . '

'Yeah I know,' she interrupts. 'Come in.'

The girl is tall and skinny with long bleached blonde hair that's unkempt to say the least. She has a pretty face, if a little long, and looks like a model. She's wearing a long green dress that shows off her ample cleavage. I sneak a glance and decide that she's not wearing a bra.

'I didn't catch your name . . . ' I say, entering a hallway with no furniture and dropping my bag on the floor by the door.

'Christie,' she says, turning her back on me and walking away into an adjacent room.

'Cool . . . ' I say, to myself.

Nervous, I walk into a larger room, which has a dining table and chairs and a small kitchen at one end, and a mattress at the other. Sitting around the table are three people: an unshaven man with greasy black hair, effortlessly cool, looks like a photographer; a youngish girl in a dressing gown, perhaps another model; and an oldish, Asian woman, probably hair and make-up. Christie is standing behind them, making some tea.

'Hi,' I say, to the room really.

'Hi,' says the man in a thick Irish accent. He promptly stands up and shakes my hand. 'Do you want something to drink, man? Some tea? I'm Danny by the way.'

'Like *Danny Boy*?' I say, laughing. 'Yeah, sure,' I say, after there's no reaction. 'Um, just some water . . . please.'

'Christie, one tea for me and some water for Alex, *please*. No sugar, thanks. I'm sweet enough.' Everyone laughs this time and he sits down, picking up a half-smoked Marlboro Light from an ash tray in front of him.

'Thanks, Christie.' I look over at her but she's not looking at me. 'So, what's the plan? I thought it was just going to be Kate and . . . ' I trail off while nodding at the girl in the gown.

'What do you mean, man?' asks Danny, frowning. 'Oh, you mean Rheanna! God no, man. She's my girl. Isn't that right Ra-Ra?' He kisses her on the cheek and she stares at me and then frowns.

'Don't call me Ra-Ra,' she says. 'I hate it when you call me Ra-Ra . . . ' She gets up and walks over to the mattress, takes off her dressing gown and climbs into bed.

'Kate is, um, busy, if you know what I mean,' says Danny, laughing. 'We'll shoot her another day.'

'You need to get ready,' says Christie, not looking at me as she places a glass of water on the table.

Danny and Christie go upstairs and I hear Christie giggle when Danny says something to her, then Rheanna gets up from the mattress, switches on the hi-fi and puts on a David Bowie CD.

Over the next half an hour or so, the make-up lady

moisturises my skin and straightens my hair before sculpting
it back off my face. Presumably happy with my appearance,
she disappears before reappearing a moment later with
Christie, who's holding some clothes.

'It's just the one look,' she says. 'You'll be wearing Bel-
staff. This jacket and some jeans and boots. Oh, and these ski
goggles.' She dumps all of this on the chair next to me.

'OK . . . ' I say as she vanishes again.

I change and Rheanna tells me to go upstairs, but when I
do nobody's there. As I walk from an empty room into a small
bathroom, wondering where everyone is, I look out of the
window and see that Danny and Christie and the make-up
lady are standing on the rooftop. I climb through the window
and join them on the makeshift terrace. We're so high up I
can practically see all of Central London.

'OK, we're looking for two shots, man,' Danny says. 'The
first is a head shot, which we'll do now. The second is an action
shot . . . '

'An action shot?' I say, interrupting him.

'Yeah, man. We've got these balloons and we're gonna try
and, like, get you jumping in the air with them . . . like they're
lifting you off into the atmosphere . . . or something . . . ' He
laughs. 'Kate's going to be the other six shots. Don't worry,
man, it'll look good . . . '

I look over at Christie, who's sitting down on an elevated
part of the rooftop. Her knees are slightly apart and her right
foot is resting on a large tripod. From where I'm standing, I
see she's not wearing any underwear and can make out the
pink of her labia, and even some dark stubble on her inner
right thigh.

'Cool . . . '

33

Four hours later, I leave the shoot. Checking my phone as I walk down Old Street, I see I have a new e-mail from Nathalie:

Alex, I know you like to hear about my day so . . . Cha-Cha came back in today and I got this e-mail from 'Lotte.

Hi all,

FYI – in case you missed today's brainstorm with Cha-Cha, here are their nine trends for '09:

- Humbition (humility plus ambition) in the workplace.
- Brand Me (branding for individuals).
- Chindia.
- Globalization of everything.
- Back to normal food.
- Redefinition of family.
- Global warming is no longer a myth.
- Reality becomes meaningless.
- Anti-social is the new normal.

As for branding, they say that future markets will be driven by 'brand sluts' – consumers who are willing to switch loyalties, flitting from one brand to another whenever a better offer comes along. A brand will be more than a designer label connected with a particular product. Instead, it will stand for an ideal or philosophy. Apple has expanded beyond computer manufacturing into music retailing through iTunes. Virgin is more than a music label; it's also an airline and a phone company. Expect to see more of these seemingly bizarre shifts. Increasingly, brands can be abstracted from the products that embody them; their essence can be distilled into an idea, a spirit that retains its power across product categories.

Regards,

Charlotte

I finish reading the e-mail as I approach Old Street underground station and see a young woman standing very still in front of the entrance. As I pass by, I notice that she's not wearing anything on her feet and is balancing a pair of old cowboy boots on her head.

34

That night, I go to a house party in Camden with Hugo. The house belongs to someone we both know vaguely from university, but we've been here half an hour and I'm already getting restless. It's not got going yet and I don't recognise anyone.

While we're drinking lukewarm beer in the kitchen, a group of boys – maybe aged eighteen or so, dressed in vintage suits with skinny ties, like they're in a band – enter the room. They're excited but circumspect, having scored some coke, and as they go to a nearby bedroom and close the door I wonder why they're being so secretive about it.

As we leave the kitchen to explore we bump into Rebecca, one of the girls living in the house and presumably responsible for this party.

'Hi guys!' she yells, throwing herself all over us. Rebecca is petite with long blonde hair and is wearing a red beret and glasses with thick black frames, even though she doesn't need them to see.

'Hi,' says Hugo. He waves sardonically but Rebecca doesn't get it, just waves back smiling.

'Yeah, great party,' I add.

'You look great, Alex!' she says, looking at me a little too intensely. 'You too Hugo,' she adds, still looking at me.

'Where's Katie?' asks Hugo. He and Katie used to go out at university and they were pretty serious, I guess. Katie and Nathalie were best friends and the four of us were inseparable. Everything we did, we did together. They split up a year ago and haven't spoken since, but when Hugo heard she might be here tonight he begged me to come. I said I would. I think they call that moral support but, hey, what are friends for?

'Haven't you heard?' says Rebecca, adopting a solemn tone. 'She failed her re-sits and dropped out. I think she's starting a film course in September, but I haven't heard from her in ages . . . ' Rebecca trails off and waves to someone across the room.

Hugo looks confused but I know, after being told by Nathalie, that Katie is working as a full frontal lap dancer in Hammersmith and definitely has no plans to go back to university.

'Oh . . . OK. No, I . . . I did not know that,' he says, after a moment. He looks around the room and sips his drink. I suddenly notice that he and I are the only boys here not wearing a tie.

'So Alex,' says Rebecca, touching my hand. 'How are you and Nathalie? I mean, are you two still together or what?'

'Alexander is fucking other people right now but yes, they're still together,' says Hugo, before I can answer.

'Um,' I say, trying to laugh, 'well, that's not strictly, um, true, but we're . . . kind of seeing each other still. I mean, we're still together, yes . . . '

'Kind of together? Not strictly true?' Hugo adopts a faux-incredulous tone and is waving his hands around while speaking really loudly.

'We're still together,' I say, again. 'Rebecca, can you please excuse us?' I drag Hugo out of the room but before we reach the door he grabs my arm.

'Alexander, I'm sorry,' he says. 'I shouldn't have said that. It's just . . . what she said . . . about Katie . . . '

'Let's go,' I say, and we leave.

35

I'm on my way to a test shoot, listening to *Happy Go-Go Lucky* by Alimo on my iPhone. As I push through the crowds in Holborn underground station, looking for an exit and scrolling through the artists to select a new song, I see I have yet another e-mail from Nathalie:

> *FYI Alex – some more cool trends because I know you think you're sooo cool!*
> *Kisses, Nathalie.*
> *p.s. See you tonight . . . ?*

Hi all,
For those of you unable to attend the conference call with L.A. on Monday, here are 50 things to look out for in '09:
  1 Skype/VoIP.
  2 Twitter.
  3 The business of social networking.
  4 Pop-up stores, restaurants and bars – installation style.
  5 Shrinky Dink technology (televisions are flat and hidden, iPods are down to half an ounce, speakers are smaller and less visible, and so on).
  6 The rise of nanotechnology.
  7 Sustainable construction/green buildings.

8 Hydrogen fuel cell technology.

9 Veggie-bus: school buses running on biodiesel fuel.

10 The continued growth of reality television talent searches.

11 Fear of agri-terrorism.

12 Halal foods.

13 Participatory advertising (user-generated advertising and music video competitions).

14 Premium drink bars.

15 Organic cotton.

16 Stem cell research.

17 Dev Patel, star of *Slumdog Millionaire*.

18 Hybrid dogs.

19 Locally sourced produce.

20 Reunions of donor insemination siblings.

21 Hitting the off button/demanding downtime.

22 Indian crossover actress Aishwarya Rai.

23 Homeschooling.

24 Natural building materials such as stone and wood.

25 Binge chilling.

26 Personalized diets.

27 Modernized tradition.

28 Alpha Moms

29 Internet television.

30 Citizen journalism.

31 RSS feeds.

32 More Google domination (Google as acquirer, and Microsoft as Google follower).

33 Mobile video.

34 Inconspicuous consumption.

35 Leona Lewis.

36 Environmental causes.

37 Companies going green.

38 Barack Obama.

39 Soft, natural hair.

40 Party planning for teens.

41 Paying for user-generated content.

42 Higher-waisted pants.

43 Co-branding (think Nike plus Apple).

44 The rebirth of raves.

45 Mashups (music, websites, everything).

46 Europeans getting fatter.

47 Multilingual cinema.

48 Looking after 'Planet Me'.

49 Age shuffling (40 is the new 20, for example).

50 Generosity.

Regards,
Charlotte

36

I'm getting ready to meet Frankie later tonight. After a long shower, I wander into my bedroom to get dressed and notice I have a text message from her. It reads: *Get pills!*

Before I can even think of a reply, my phone rings. It's Nathalie.

'Hi,' I say, looking through my wardrobe and deciding what to wear.

'Hi,' she says, sounding pissed off.

'What's wrong?' I ask, dropping my towel and putting on some boxers.

'Are you coming over tonight?'

'Um, well . . . ' I say, struggling to balance my phone while putting on a pair of skinny jeans.

'Look, is now not a good time or something?' she says, after a moment. She sighs. 'It seems like you never have time for me anymore.'

'Well, actually,' I say, 'I'm just on my way out . . . '

'Oh yeah?' she interrupts.

'Um, how about we meet tomorrow for lunch, before I go to Paris?'

'Fine. Call me tomorrow.' She hangs up.

37

I'm having drinks in Annex 3 with Frankie and two of her male model friends. I've met them before at castings in London. The rude German is still as rude as ever.

A lounge cover of Joy Division's *Love Will Tear Us Apart* is playing and the rude German asks Brad, a Canadian surfer-type and insufferable know-it-all, who the song is by. Brad pauses – clearly not aware of who did the original – and decides to blag it anyway.

'This . . . is a cover of a Clash song,' he says assertively. 'The original is a really hard punk song, though.'

I want to shout out: 'You had to blag it, didn't you? You fucking know-it-all! You couldn't just say you weren't sure and ask anyone else if they knew, you fucking idiot!'

But instead, I simply smile and say nothing.

38

'Can I ask you a question?' says Frankie, her expression suddenly changing from jovial to earnest. We're in another bar and finally alone because the rude German and Brad are talking to some other male models outside. I nod and take a sip of my drink. 'What have you always wanted to do in bed that you've never done?'

Surprised by her question, I think for a moment, run through how many times a girl has asked me that in my head, come to a total of zero, smile.

'I'm not sure . . . '

'Come on!' she says, a little loudly. 'I don't believe you . . . '

'I'm thinking!' I protest. 'I don't know . . . why, what's yours?'

'There's nothing I've ever wanted to do that I've not done, honey,' she says, straight-faced.

I take another sip of my drink and think about the time I tried to encourage Nathalie to get it on with me and one of her friends at a party, and how that did not go down too well.

'How about a threesome?' I venture.

'Hmm . . . ' she says, smiling. 'I thought you'd say that.'

39

At 1 a.m. we go to Aura and get in free because Frankie knows everyone on the London club scene and even though the drinks are ridiculously expensive and the DJ is awful and the dance floor is full of middle-aged Arab men smoking cigars and groups of lads who've all paid way too much to go to a club where they won't pull it's OK because we have a table and we actually dance on top of it at one point.

By the time we do venture out onto the dance floor we've all had way too much £150-a-bottle Grey Goose and they're all doing pills but I don't care because I'm dancing with Frankie to the Victoria's Secret Remix of *When You Were Young* by The Killers and it's as if we're somewhere else just us and the voice of Brandon Flowers over the ethereal beat grabs hold of us and the euphoria runs through my veins and I think of Nathalie and in that moment am convinced that her feelings far outweigh mine and that what we had can be exposed in those brief but vivid moments of anguish of sheer dread in which we tearfully concluded that to be together was better than being alone and as I think of this in a daze I hold Frankie against me and we spin in the centre of the dance floor and it feels like everything's going to be OK.

We are not really here.

40

I spend the next day packing for the shows. My Eurostar to Paris is at 5 p.m. and Andreas, who's also going, is already packed.

'Hey man you need to really hurry, OK?' he says from the other room. It's his first time and he's so excited he's been pacing up and down for hours.

'Yeah, I'm nearly done,' I answer. 'Fuck off . . . ' I mumble.

'Hey, I heard that . . . '

My phone rings. It's Nathalie.

'Hi,' she says, sounding upset. 'Are you packed?'

'Hi,' I say. 'Sorry . . . I didn't hear that last part.'

'Are you packed?' she says, her voice much louder now.

'Yeah. Well, almost . . . '

'So I assume we're not meeting today then?'

'Um, well . . . I'm not packed yet and, um, I have more to do than I thought . . . '

'Alex?' she says, interrupting.

'Yes Nathalie . . . '

'If you meet anyone, while you're away . . . I mean, if you want to be with someone . . . in Milan . . . or Paris . . . '

'Nathalie, you don't need to . . . '

'If you meet a girl,' she interrupts again, 'can you please call me?'

There's a pause as I consider this, thinking about us, about Frankie, about the time I caught Nathalie with a boy in the VIP section of Café de Paris.

'I'll call you from Paris,' I say. 'I promise.' I hang up.

41

We arrive in Paris just after 8 p.m. local time and catch a cab to our hotel which is a Novotel in Parmentier and full of models hanging around in the lobby queuing for the payphone taking up all the lifts and our room's on the fourth floor and has one bedroom with two single beds and a lounge with a pullout and at check in we were told we'll be sharing with another boy who's yet to arrive so we dump our bags in the bedroom and go out to a nearby supermarket to buy pizzas and beers which we then take back to the room and by 11 p.m. he's still not turned up but that's probably a good thing because we've ended up in the lounge sprawled across the pull-out watching German MTV and drinking cheap Belgian beers and contemplating falling asleep.

42

After a breakfast of black coffee and cigarettes, we make our way to our agency, which is in the centre of Le Marais in a small courtyard opposite another agency. We're buzzed in and upstairs, through a small waiting room, there's another small room with four bookers positioned around a large desk. A small fluffy dog is running around and jumping up at my booker, Veronique, an oldish lady with big blonde hair and large glasses with yellow frames.

'Bonjour, me again,' I say, approaching the desk.

'Ah bonjour, Alexander, ça va?' says Veronique, kissing me on both cheeks as I stand over her. She stands up slowly and greets Andreas in similar fashion.

'You must meet Bailey,' she says. 'Come, we go outside.' She steers us back into the waiting room where there's a boy waiting alone. 'This is Bailey,' she says. 'Bailey, this is Alexander and Andreas. You will share a room.'

He stands up and looks me up and down, as if weighing me up, before shaking my hand. I recognise him from somewhere. He's very slim and very handsome, with short brown hair that's shaved close at the sides, hollow cheeks and bright blue eyes. He's wearing a tight-fitting Ramones T-shirt, skinny jeans and a pair of battered winklepickers.

'Hey,' I say. 'We must've walked right past you . . . ' I laugh and he just looks at me blankly.

'Bailey,' Veronique interrupts, 'you will leave your bag 'ere and go to castings with Alexander and Andreas. Do you all 'ave maps?' We all nod. 'OK, do not forget to check in at the end of the day,' she says, turning away and walking back to her desk. 'Bonne chance!'

43

The three of us are walking down Avenue George V and as we pass a refuse truck I pinch my nose and look away because of the smell and I see the words *Pas de replâtrage la structure est pourrie* sprayed in red graffiti above a café.

When we arrive at Givenchy, it seems like every boy in Paris is waiting in the lobby. There are black boys with dreadlocks and push bikes and American boys who carry skate boards and look like tourists in shorts and sandals and beautiful Brazilian boys all doing weird handshakes and talking loudly to one another.

Eventually, a few of us are asked to walk through a court-yard to a large studio room, where we wait again. Half an hour passes, maybe longer, and then it's my turn. After demonstrating that I can walk without smiling while keeping my chin down, I hand my book to a French-looking girl and a Japanese-looking boy. The boy stares at me but doesn't say a word and, after taking my card, the girl says 'Thank you' and I leave.

I tell Andreas I'll wait for him but he doesn't hear me because he's laughing at something Bailey's telling him. On the pavement in front of the building, I light a cigarette and think about calling Nathalie. Instead, I call Frankie.

'Hi, what's up?' she answers, sounding distracted and not that happy to hear from me.

'Hi Frankie, um . . . well, I'm in Paris and I thought I'd give you a call and, um . . . so, what's up?' As I say this, I try my best to sound casual.

'Oh nothing, just . . . I'm just doing some shopping . . . ' I can hear someone talking to her but can't make out what they're saying. I'm convinced it's a boy.

'Are you with someone?' I ask. 'I can call later if you want . . . '

'No . . . I mean, yes,' she says, laughing. 'Can you call later?'

I say I will and hang up.

44

It's hot today and I'm with Andreas outside a Tabac, waiting for Bailey to buy cigarettes and a Coke. We're running late for the last casting of the day, for Dior, and I know it will be a waste of time because I'm not fifteen and worse still, it's back near where we were this morning for Yves Saint-Laurent, over on the other side of town, which is annoying to say the least.

At the casting, we're all sitting on long white pews in a small room with high ceilings and white walls. After a while, around ten of us are called into another room, which is almost identical but without the pews. There are five people in there – four men and one woman – and they ask us to put our books down against a wall and stand side by side. They then proceed to walk along the line, starting from the far side, and two of the first three boys are asked to leave. The rest of us are asked to walk around the room, single file, and after we've walked around the room three times they say 'Thank you' in unison and then pull one boy aside. He's very young-looking, maybe fourteen, with long blonde hair tied back in a pony-tail. He's so pretty he could easily pass for a girl.

As I walk out of the room, they all gather around the boy, nodding inanely to one another and writing on clipboards, obsessing over him, touching his hair and asking him to pull it back off his face.

45

Even though we've had castings for five days straight and fly to Milan tomorrow, Bailey's convinced us to go out with him and two really young-looking female models he met in our hotel. In a café on Avenue de la République, we're all drinking litres of beer while he tells us about his career so far.

'It all started last season,' he tells us in between sips of his beer, his full red lips wrapped around the bottle's thick shaft. 'I was in my last year at high school back in Burlington – that's in Canada, where I'm from – and I was scouted in the mall and I found myself spending the winter in Paris, Milan and London. I'd never been to Europe – I'd never even left Burlington. It was crazy . . . '

I've heard all of this before. Earlier today, when we were

waiting for a casting for Issey Miyake and lying on the grass in Place des Vosges, I realised where I recognised him from. We met last season in Milan. We were both doing the Calvin Klein show and talked while we had our make-up done, although clearly he doesn't remember.

'I did thirty-four shows last season in Milan, Paris and New York, and then Marc Jacobs flew me to London for Fashion Week,' he says, looking at me. 'Last week, I was in L.A. at the Mondrian, doing a shoot for *Details*, and now I'm in Paris. It's awesome . . . '

I stifle a yawn and look at the girls, who are talking among themselves. As Bailey continues, still looking at me, I take a large gulp of beer and glance at Andreas, who's listening intently, his mouth slightly ajar.

After we've finished our third and done shots of tequila that make me feel sick, we end up in a gay bar in Le Marais because one of the girls said 'You must see this!' and when we get to the bar we all order vodka pomme and stand in the middle of a small dance floor, not dancing, while loud music plays and butch men stare at us, and I recognise a few models from castings and wonder whether they're here for the same reason as us.

We're not in the bar long before everyone turns around, and only then do I notice a glass box in the wall with a naked man showering, not facing us. He's very muscular and his buttocks seem enormous to me. I look over at Andreas and the girls, who are all laughing, and for a moment I can't see Bailey. The man washes himself awkwardly and bends over, spreading his arse cheeks so we can all see his pink arsehole, before turning around and stroking his huge penis, which is thick, the size of the litre beer bottles we were drinking from earlier. I turn around and Bailey is behind me, smiling and holding out another vodka pomme. I say 'Thanks' and turn to watch the showering man. As he strains his muscular body with every

72

pose, his expression is plaintive, even embarrassed, and I can only stare, trying to empathise.

At some point in the early hours, Andreas, Bailey and I ditch the girls and catch a cab back to our hotel. As soon as he gets through the door, Andreas flops on the pull-out in the lounge, which is Bailey's bed, and is out like a light. It's quite dark in the room but I can still make out Bailey, standing in the hall. I look at him and he looks at me for a moment.

'Um, do you want a beer? I might get one . . . ' I say, closing the lounge door and walking past him to the fridge in the kitchen.

'I'm gonna take a shower, man,' he says, grabbing my arm. 'Wanna join me?' He lets go of my arm and takes off his Ramones T-shirt to reveal a very slim but muscled torso, his skin pale and smooth. He licks his lips and steps back, allowing me to admire his well-defined chest and arms, his cubed abs. He then drops his jeans so that he's only wearing a pair of white briefs and walks over to the bathroom door, before taking them off. Looking back at me over his shoulder, he smiles. 'I said, wanna join me?'

46

The next morning, Andreas, Bailey and I are waiting to board a plane to Milan. They're both listening to iPods and I'm checking my phone for messages while watching CNN on mute. It's been days since I last talked to Frankie and when I call I just get her voicemail.

On the television, an advert for a financial services company comes on.

High performance. Delivered.

47

It's late afternoon by the time we land and after altering our watches and collecting our luggage we catch a bus from the airport into the city centre.

Milan is a city with only a few tall buildings, all of which have huge advertising billboards on the top. When we get into the centre, we split up because Bailey's with a different agency in Milan. He says 'See you around' before jumping on the Metro, and I pull out my map and decide that Andreas and I need a tram to get to our agency on the other side of the city.

The agency is on Via Vincenzo Monti, a tree-lined street that is almost identical to every other in Milan. After jumping off the tram without paying and eventually finding the right building, we walk through a courtyard to what looks like a back entrance, get in a lift with a couple of female models, ask them why they're in town during castings for menswear shows and then part company as we wander into men's division.

'Ciao Alexander!' says Maria, our booker. Maria's über Italian-looking – attractive and tan – and as we approach her desk she stands up to kiss me on both cheeks. 'Welcome back to Milano.'

'Hello,' says Andreas, also kissing her on both cheeks.

'You both need cards so wait here for, ah, uno minuto,' she says.

'Where do you want us to put our bags?' I ask, sitting down at her desk.

'You can, ah, leave them there until later,' she says, gesturing at an area at the back of the room. 'You have a casting for Jil Sander, then you can go to your hotel.'

She leaves the room and returns again after a moment, handing us each a pile of cards. Mine say 'Alexander W' underneath a headshot of me that was taken during one of my first shoots, for *i-D*.

'Andreas, I see you have, ah, red marks,' she says, pointing at her own chin. 'Do you have any, ah, concealer? If not, I can give you some. If you get a spot you need to cover it, OK?' Andreas nods, blushing. 'And do you have a map?'

'I have one,' I interrupt. 'We'll be together, right?'

'OK, good. Andreas, you will stay with Alexander and go to the same castings. Keep together. In Milan it is, ah, very easy to get lost.'

48

We make our way across the city on the Metro, which is full of very young but very pretty girls who just stare at us and giggle.

When we arrive at the casting, just after 4.30 p.m., it doesn't look good. We're made to wait around in a large room full of other boys and, despite the call sheet saying the casting is from 4 p.m. until 5 p.m., they seem to have taken a break because nothing's happening.

An hour or so passes before a man wearing dark sunglasses enters the room, accompanied by three or four other people hovering around him. He's holding a grey suit jacket and, after standing there for a moment, he looks at me and gestures with his finger for me to come over. He holds out the jacket for me to try on, still without saying a word, and I comply. After turning me around and stepping back to look at how it fits, he smiles as if to say I'm no longer needed, so I take off the jacket and go back to my seat.

We leave the casting at 7 p.m. and go back across Milan to the agency to pick up our bags. After getting back on the Metro with our bags and going back across the city, we walk for what feels like a long time through empty streets lined with derelict buildings and closed shops covered in graffiti, and it's a miracle that we find our hotel.

There are large groups of models outside smoking cigarettes and standing in the reception and just sitting around doing nothing. Andreas spots a boy he knows from home and starts talking to him in German while we check in. I leave him to it and go upstairs to our room because I'm so tired.

When I wake up, at around 10 p.m., I'm alone. I check my phone for messages and see that I have one from Nathalie, one from my dad and none from Frankie. I think about calling Frankie but then change my mind and take a quick shower, watch German MTV for an hour and fall asleep.

49

It's so hot in Milan and Andreas and I spend the next few days going to ten castings a day for Alexander McQueen and Burberry and Calvin Klein and Costume National and Dirk Bikkembergs and Dolce & Gabbana and DSquared and Etro and Gianfranco Ferré and Giorgio Armani and Gucci and Iceberg and M + F Girbaud and Marni and Missoni and Moschino and Neil Barrett and Prada and Roberto Cavalli and Romeo Gigli and Valentino and Versace and Vivienne Westwood with models that all look the same and by the third day Andreas is spending a lot of time with his German friend and other young models in the hotel playing Play Station and smoking joints all night and he tells me he wants to go to castings on his own.

By the fifth day, I feel lost and am forced to seek solace in areas I'd normally avoid: I watch quiz shows on the English language station in the hotel room; I take photographs of ubiquitous corporate chains; I buy chocolate you can get in London, even though I don't like it.

Consumed by exaggerated thoughts of my grief, boredom,

loneliness, I am only able to pretend, to hover over my feelings. Pretend to be happy, interested. Pretend to be fine.

You're one too? I knew it!

In a strange way, however, Milan is a lot like home. I saw a beggar near the hotel today and he had a pet rabbit and was feeding it lettuce. There are television screens showing adverts on street corners, on the facades of buildings, even across from the platform on the Metro. Models are everywhere.

It's true what they say. Places do begin to look the same after a while.

50

On the last day of castings, Maria pulls me into a small room at the agency. Before I can sit down in front of the small desk, expecting the worst, she hugs me.

'Alexander,' she says, still hugging me, 'you remember how well you did last time? You did, ah, four shows, correct? That was, ah, very good for your first season, you understand? Without pictures and, ah . . . '

'Yes I remember,' I interrupt, stepping back so we're face to face. 'Why?'

'Well, do you know how many shows you got this season?' she says, grinning inanely and flashing white teeth between shiny lips.

'Um, no . . . but you're going to tell me, right?' I say, letting out a laugh.

'You got ten shows!' she yells, and then she hugs me again, this time tighter.

51

It's Milan Fashion Week and on the first day I do fittings for Alexander McQueen, Calvin Klein, DSquared, Etro, Gucci and Missoni, and I just wait around for hours while dozens of other boys try on trousers and jackets and corsets and are paraded in front of the designer, before it's my turn.

That evening, I have a showroom for Ermenegildo Zegna, which is essentially a private show in the boutique for clients and hand-picked journalists. I'm with another boy, who's from Switzerland and looks exactly like me. Other than saying 'Hi' when we meet in the back to get changed and despite the fact we spend half the time getting ready, he doesn't talk to me all evening.

It doesn't bother me, though. After all, we spend two hours in total walking around the perimeter of a small room and are each paid 1,000 euros for our efforts.

52

On day three, after shows for Burberry, Costume National and Prada, I'm out having dinner in a hybrid Chinese-Italian restaurant with three male models who I know from London and bumped into at the Gucci fitting. They're talking about the girls in Milan.

'I agree they're hot, but have you seen the old women here? That's what they'll turn into!' says Patrick, a handsome blonde boy with a New Romantic haircut, high cheekbones and full lips. 'Anyone else want one?' he asks, after ordering a beer from a passing waiter.

'Yeah, get another round in, mate,' says Jono. Jono used

to be a builder and looks the part, with a shaved head and a thick cockney accent. He's the only person I know who can start a story with 'I was fisting this bird with factor 15 sun cream . . . ' and he only got into modelling by accident. He was working in a building while a casting was going on, and the casting agents liked him so much they booked him on the spot. He had to find an agency just to do the shoot. 'They're fit in Milan,' he continues, staring at me and grinning, 'but I reckon the birds at 'ome are buffer.'

'No way,' says Patrick, 'and what's more, they all love models here.'

'That's true,' adds Rupert, a pretty boy who I think is at university in Oxford. 'Think about it. The men here hate us because they know, every time we come to town, we're shagging all their women!'

Patrick bursts out laughing and high fives Rupert.

'Mate, if you reckon they're a bit of alright 'ere you should go to Thailand,' says Jono. 'Wall to wall birds and if you've got baht, you can get anything you want. You can get one on your cock, one on your face, one with your fingers in her . . . '

The waiter interrupts by bringing another round of beers.

'What do you think, Alex?' says Patrick, after a moment. 'Don't you have a girlfriend?'

'You an egg 'n' chips man, Alex?' Jono interrupts, laughing. 'Fuck that. My motto's simple: train hard, save dough, fuck birds, smash baddies.'

The table erupts.

53

I'm doing the Gucci show today and I arrive on time, just, having done the Alexander McQueen show at noon.

Hungry and tired, I go with Jono, Patrick and Rupert to

grab some food from the canteen, which we share with local builders doing work on a nearby college. The builders stare at us threateningly as we help ourselves to mixed salad and Coke, but Jono thinks they're good-looking and could probably model if they wanted to.

I have two outfits, which I'm shown to by a couple of Japanese girls. The second outfit is just a classic silver suit with a white shirt and white shoes that I tried on at the fitting, but I've never seen the first outfit before. It's a cropped turquoise hoodie, some grey shorts that leave nothing to the imagination and a pair of sandals. When I slip on the shorts to try them, the Japanese girls giggle and this makes me frown, so they stop.

There's an hour to go and we all get changed in a small pre-fab building adjacent to a large assembly room, which is where the show will be, and it's really hot inside and looks like it's been constructed for one day only, and as we undress I notice that all of the other boys wear white briefs and I study them, comparing their physiques to mine.

A black DJ with a silver wig plays *Notorious* by Duran Duran as I walk down the catwalk, nearly slipping in the ridiculous sandals, then I'm rushed backstage to do a change and no sooner have I stepped out of the sandals than the Japanese girls roughly take off my hoodie and pull down my shorts, so I'm standing naked waiting for them to help me with the trousers, and I say 'While you're down there . . . ' and grin but they don't understand, and then there's a panic when one of them thinks I've split the trousers of the suit but the other decides I haven't and everyone seems relieved.

Once a little powder is applied, I'm back out on the catwalk, this time to a dance remix of *Money For Nothing* by Dire Straits.

I want my . . .
I want my . . .
I want my MTV . . .

54

After ten days in Milan, I can't wait to leave. I've only just got back to the hotel after doing the Calvin Klein show earlier and my flight to Paris is at 3 p.m., but I've not packed yet.

In the room, I'm trying to gather my things while Andreas lies on my bed, half naked, smoking yet another joint. Our agency in Paris called last night to tell him he didn't get any shows, so he's decided to stay in Milan for a few weeks. He's spent the last couple of days lounging around in the hotel, stoned, and there's something different about him.

'Look man, you've got to get out of my way or I'll miss my flight,' I say, trying to drag him off the bed by his right leg. 'I need to pack this stuff and you're lying all over it.'

'Blow me,' he says, laughing.

'Come on . . . ' I say, exasperated.

'No seriously,' he says, pulling his boxers down to show me his semi.

'If I blow you, will you pack?' I ask, straight-faced.

'What, like you did to Bailey? Fucking faggot . . . ' he says, pulling his shorts back up and getting off the bed. 'Happy now?'

55

I land in Paris and after catching a train to Gare du Nord I jump on the Metro and go straight to my agency and when I arrive I kiss the bookers on both cheeks including the guys and Veronique is excited because I have eight shows and I say 'I'm excited too' and this makes her smile and then I get back on the Metro to go to my hotel which is now a 4-star and after checking in and being shown to my room I end up falling asleep because I'm so tired.

56

At around midnight, Frankie finally calls, waking me up. She tells me she can't come to Paris because she's busy. I don't bother to tell her that she wasn't invited or to ask what she could possibly be busy doing.

Instead, I simply tell her I'll call when I get back to London in four days.

57

I spend day one doing fittings for Comme des Garçons, Dries van Noten, Givenchy, Jean-Paul Gaultier, Paul Smith, Sonia Rykiel and Yves Saint-Laurent. I was going to be exclusive for YSL again but Veronique knew I'd make more money doing other shows as well so she turned them down.

The shows are all tomorrow and I'm really tired after Milan, but it was the right decision.

58

On day three, I'm at John Galliano in eastern Paris. I'm here for the fitting and also to act as a mannequin for the make-up artists because they want to get everything right before tonight's show.

In the morning, a few other male models and I take turns having make-up applied and Polaroids taken in between eating fruit and not talking to one another. One boy, an African with very dark skin and a chiselled torso, is sprayed with Evian by two giggling Japanese girls, enhancing his already well-defined chest and abdomen.

After lunch, when it's my turn to try on my outfit, I walk into a large room with a long table, behind which sit four men and one woman. In the corner of the room, on a smaller table, sits the designer.

I'm told to put on my one outfit for the show – a black waistcoat, a pair of low-slung blue jeans over Galliano print underwear, white cowboy boots and a silver top hat – and after I've walked for the people in the room the designer decides I look better without the waistcoat and discards his creation, before going back to his solitary position in the corner.

I'm asked to leave.

59

Later that evening, tired from fittings and shows and taking cabs backwards and forwards across town, I make my way to an industrial estate in the Parisian suburbs for tonight's show. My call time is 6 p.m., but I know it won't start until around 9 so turn up at 7.30 p.m. instead.

I give my name to a security guard on the door of a large warehouse and am ushered into hair and make-up, which is in a corner of what is essentially one huge open-plan space. There are around forty models and what feels like twice as many make-up artists, stylists, assistants and other assorted fashionistas buzzing around.

After half an hour or so of having black eye shadow and purple nail varnish applied, I help myself to the feast of baguettes, assorted cheeses and meats and piles of fresh fruit that have been laid out at the back of the room while talking to a really big model I know from the Paul Smith show.

On the opposite side to the food are racks of clothes, in front of which sit models – some reading, some talking, one playing a guitar. While finishing an entire carton of pomegranate juice, I make my way past the outfits to the one with a Polaroid of me attached to it. I ask a passing Japanese girl when the show's going to start, and she says 'Ah . . . maybe one hour?' so I sit down on the floor and pull out a copy of *Nausea*.

I borrowed it from Nathalie a year ago but so far I've not managed to get beyond the first chapter.

60

Most of the models are getting ready now and the makeshift changing area is open and as well as what looks like a stylist per outfit I notice a group of young girls just standing around and watching us undress and as I strip naked to put on my outfit starting with a pair of Galliano briefs which is a full outfit for some boys I wink at one girl who's looking me up and down and then I ask a stylist if she could get me some more pomegranate juice.

Once we're all changed we get into line and Japanese girls and fruity men fuss until we're in the correct order and I'm in between two Brazilian boys talking loudly to one another and I watch as a really tall girl with a huge bleached blonde beehive on her head who's opening the show starts panicking because her right stiletto keeps opening and two Japanese girls rush to help her and then she's dragged to the front of the line by two men wearing earpieces and holding two-way radios.

All of a sudden I hear someone talking through a mega-phone and when I look at the entrance to the stage up ahead I can see the creative director and just about hear him as he instructs us in bad English to keep our chins down and walk with attitude and then the lights go down and a jazz band starts playing *Mr. Bojangles* and we all watch the screen as the show begins and one by one the models walk and the girl loses her shoe almost immediately but glides down the catwalk without it and a man standing next to me wearing an earpiece yells in what sounds like an American accent 'It doesn't matter people she still looked *fierce!*' and just before it's my turn to step out onto the catwalk the designer who's standing in the doorway wearing a pink suit and a silver top hat like mine says 'You look great!' and I walk.

61

On a high after the show, a few of us catch a cab to the Champs Élysées for a Fashion Week after-party hosted by our agency.

When we arrive, we're shown to a table and all night beautiful male waiters keep bringing trays of spirits and mixers with fireworks on top of the bottles, and after a while I start to wonder why I'm here.

I go with the flow and, after drinking too much vodka, do pills in the toilets with a bunch of male models. They end up kissing in the cubicle, which surprises me a little as the pills are having no effect on me whatsoever.

When I find my way back to our table, I focus my attention on a French girl called Juliette who's with a model from the show. She's petite with caramel hair that's tied back loosely and, in this light, she looks beautiful. I stare at her full red lips as she talks to me about her boyfriend and her poor English, which is actually really good and certainly better than my Franglais.

'We 'ave, 'ow you say . . . we are together three years,' she tells me with her hand resting on my knee.

'And what do you think of English boys?' I ask, quite drunk by now and moving closer so I can feel her breath on my face as she speaks.

'I like them because I can practice my English!' She laughs and pushes me lightly on the shoulder.

I check my watch. It's 1.30 a.m. Time to leave, I decide, and I whisper something disgusting in her ear that makes her giggle and we slip out of the club and onto the Champs Élysées.

After sharing a cab back to my hotel, Juliette tells me she's hungry and I say 'Look in the mini-bar' and she says 'Très cher, non?' and I say 'Don't worry about it' and we set about emptying it, devouring two tubes of Pringles, a large Toblerone, six small cans of Heineken and four tiny bottles of Veuve Clicquot.

Later, standing by the window smoking a joint, Juliette tells me about her boyfriend and how she knows he cheats on her. I say 'I don't care' but she says 'I want to explain' and so I say 'You're boring me now' and she laughs.

We lie back on my bed together and smoke cigarettes until we fall asleep. When I wake up, only a few hours later, she's gone but has left a note:

You are a beautiful sleeper. Find me if you visit in Paris again. Bonne chance. Juliette x

62

I arrive back in London later that afternoon. When I get home, I find that I have three missed calls and two messages from my dad. He doesn't really say anything, merely reiterates that he's been trying to call me.

After sleeping for a few hours, I tidy my flat, which is a lot easier with Andreas away. Once I've cleaned the front room, I walk into the bathroom and it looks filthy so I clean that too.

Later, I take a long shower and wash my hair twice, before spraying on a new re-energising serum I picked up in Paris for 120 euros because a boy who did the Dries van Noten show with me recommended it. Wrapped in a towel, I wander into the kitchen and grab some juice from the fridge before relaxing in front of the television but, after an hour of watching *Big Brother* while trying to masturbate over Juliette, I can't stand it anymore and decide to go out for a drink.

I call Frankie but she's still not answering her phone. I try Hugo. I've not heard from him in weeks and he sounds down. We arrange to meet at Loungelover in an hour.

63

On the bus going along Bethnal Green Road, there's a sticker with the words *Jesus saves sinners repent and be saved* over an advert for shampoo that says *SO CITRUSSY, YOU WON'T KNOW WHETHER TO WASH WITH IT OR DRINK IT.*

I arrive at Loungelover a little early but a table for two is free. A tall South African girl with cropped black hair and red lipstick leads me through a bar area that looks like a taxidermist's wet dream – animal heads on the walls surround space age furniture upon which ambivalent-looking arty types sit, a rusted chandelier hanging over them and a giant Ming vase in the corner – and I'm sure the people behind this must be gay.

I ask a passing waiter, who looks like he could probably model, to bring me a Zatoichi, which is wasabi, ginger and cucumber shaken with lemon and Polstar cucumber vodka, served straight up in a Martini glass. Hugo arrives at the same time as my drink.

'Hi,' he says, looking glum.

'Great to see you too,' I reply. 'He'll have the same, please,' I say to the waiter. Hugo, who's wearing his trademark blue Paul Smith suit without a tie look, sits down opposite me.

'What's up?' I ask, after a moment.

'Oh nothing,' he says. 'Look I'm sorry. I don't mean to be . . . it's just . . . '

A pause.

'Yes . . . ?' I say, hoping he'll finish his sentence.

'You look great by the way. Did you get a tan out in Paris?' He smiles and punches me on the shoulder.

'Come on, what's up?' I ask.

'OK OK . . . ' he says, pausing again while the waiter delivers his drink and then disappears. 'I heard from Katie today.'

'Oh,' I manage, after a moment.

'She told me to stop calling her parents, asking about her. I told her I'd tell her dad about her new job and . . . '

'You didn't?' I interrupt. 'Come on Hugo, you can't . . . '

'Of course I can!' he says, raising his voice. 'This is a man who visits prostitutes his daughter's age. He'll understand where I'm coming from.' I sip my drink and think of all the times I've had to deal with the fall-out from Hugo and Katie. 'Don't get your knickers in a twist,' he continues, after another moment. 'I don't need to threaten her.'

'Um, and why's that?' I ask.

'Because I know where she works and we're going tonight. This is terrible by the way,' he says, pointing at his drink.

64

We're in a cab to the place where Katie works but I'm confused because we seem to be heading east and I'm sure Nathalie told me Katie was working in Hammersmith.

'What's the matter with you?' Hugo says, looking out of the window.

'Um, nothing, it's just . . . um . . . I don't understand where we're going . . . '

'We're going to see Katie, remember? But first we're picking up Louis. He's still burning the midnight oil.'

Louis is one of Hugo's work buddies. I've only met him a few times but, put simply, he's a twat.

We pull up to a large office building and Louis is standing outside. He's wearing a blue pinstripe suit and talking on his mobile while smoking a cigarette. When he spots us, he ends the call and drops the cigarette in a nearby drain, before getting into the cab, shaking hands with Hugo and briefly nodding at me.

'How's the posing going?' he asks sarcastically, I think.

'You just got back from Paris and Milan, didn't you Alexander?' Hugo interrupts, still looking out of the window. 'He made a shit load . . . '

This shuts Louis up and he looks out of the window. After driving across town in silence, we finally arrive at Vixens in Hammersmith and I'm relieved for some reason.

We walk up to what looks like a typical dive before entering through two large doors, in front of which stand two security guards who seem to be doing nothing. Inside is one large room. There's a pretty ordinary bar to our left, a seating area on the other side where groups of middle-aged men congregate, and a small stage at the front. There's a DJ booth next to the stage with a small fat man, presumably the DJ, sitting inside. At the back of the room, opposite the stage, is a small doorway with tassels hanging down, concealing a private room.

Rough-looking Eastern European girls are walking around the room, wearing cheap-looking lingerie and holding out old-fashioned pint glasses. As two of them walk past, Hugo drops three pound coins in and they smile and walk away.

I can't see Katie and think to myself that this is a good thing, that we can just have a laugh, and after Hugo brings some drinks over to the table where Louis and I sit in silence, the night seems to go OK for an hour or so until an oldish blonde girl comes over.

'You boys up for some private dancing?' she says, in a thick Polish accent.

'No thanks darling,' says Louis, laughing. The girl looks disappointed.

'How about you?' she says to me, regaining her composure.

'Um, no . . . I mean . . . no thanks,' I manage.

'Come on, you know you would like to fuck me,' she says, out of nowhere.

'Oi oi! Go on Alex, you're in there!' says Louis, grabbing my shoulder.

'No thanks,' I say, blushing and removing his hand from my shoulder. The girl just shrugs and walks away.

As Louis takes the piss out of me, I look over Hugo's shoulder and see Katie by the bar. She's obviously just started and is doing the rounds with a pint glass.

'Have you seen that girl on stage now?' I say, looking at Hugo. 'She's, um . . . fit. Why don't you two go on up there and get us a closer spot? I'll get another round in.'

'Can't turn that one down, mate,' says Louis. 'I mean, you being a supermodel and all . . . '

Hugo and Louis walk over to a table next to the stage and watch as a naked girl bends over, spreading her legs and making her arsehole pulsate. I go over to where Katie's standing at the bar.

'Hi,' I say, not sure how she'll react. I haven't seen her in over a year and the last time didn't go well at all.

'Are you here with Hugo?' she asks, looking around the room anxiously. I say nothing, which she realises means 'Yes' and causes her to grab my hand and drag me into the private room. 'What the fuck?' she yells, throwing me on some dirty-looking red seating in front of a pole. I notice the room is empty. Looking at her as she paces up and down in front of me, I realise she's only wearing a g-string and tassels on her nipples. She looks gorgeous, as ever, and is definitely out of place in here.

'Um . . . ' I manage, eventually.

'Well?' she says, cutting me off. 'Is he here for me, or is this just a horrible coincidence?'

'He's here for you, but he hasn't seen you . . . yet . . . '

'Why did you come here with him?' she yells angrily. 'You knew I worked here. I told Nathalie so she'd tell you, and so you'd know where *not* to bring Hugo for one of your boys' nights out.'

'The plan was working well,' I say, trying to laugh. 'But he found out . . . um, not from me, but . . . '

An old man enters the room with another dancer, which prompts Katie to start dancing. She teases me by lifting her leg athletically above her head and tapping her pussy through her panties, and I feel uncomfortable, which is a first for me in such circumstances. As she climbs on top of me, I feel myself getting aroused and start to smile at her.

'Don't get any fucking ideas, Alex,' she says in a low voice as she grinds against my crotch.

'What's *that* supposed to mean?' I say, faux-hurt.

'I mean, *I* learn from my mistakes. You do know what that means don't you? Or is that too much to get your head around when you're walking and pouting at the same time?'

'Whoa! That's unnecessary. I'm here to help. What do you want me to do?'

'Stop getting a hardon?'

I look down at my crotch and regret wearing my new slim-fitting 7 For All Mankind jeans.

'OK,' I say, covering myself. 'And, um, other than that . . . ?'

Katie's about to take off her thong but before she gets to the good stuff, the old man and the dancer leave.

'You need to get Hugo out of here,' she says, turning

around to face me. 'I'm going to powder my nose. I'll give you five minutes.' She starts to walk away but stops. 'Thanks Alex,' she says, not facing me.

'Um, any time . . . '

She walks away and, after adjusting myself, I go back to Hugo and Louis by the stage.

'Hugo, I've been in that private room and there's no sign of her,' I say, standing in between them while they watch a naked brunette girl wrapping her muscular thighs around a poll. 'Why don't we get out of here?'

'Are you sure you haven't seen her?' says Hugo, not looking at me.

'Yeah, um . . . of course . . . I mean . . . '

'This place is a dump,' says Louis, interrupting me. 'I think Alex is right. Ha, I never thought I'd say that . . . '

'OK gents,' says Hugo, downing his beer. 'Let's get out of here.'

65

I'm listening to *Seventeen* by Ladytron on my iPhone as I leave Oxford Circus and walk down Argyll Street and it's also playing in a Starbucks on Great Marlborough Street, but I just shrug it off and buy a latte before changing the song and heading to my agency.

They only want you when you're seventeen,
When you're twenty-one, you're no fun.

I walk upstairs and grumble to myself about the lack of a lift, before saying 'Hi' to the cute receptionist with bad skin and walking into men's division to see Jo.

'Hi,' I say, exhausted.

'Oh look, it's our little supermodel!' she says, getting up and kissing me on both cheeks. 'How were the shows babes?'

'Oh, y'know . . . good, I guess . . . ' I say, breathing rapidly and struggling to stand because I'm so tired.

'You should be more excited, Alex,' says Sam from across the large desk. 'Look at this.' She hands me a copy of *Dazed & Confused* and I'm on the cover with Kate Moss. As I frown and think about how they managed to create the shot, Sam laughs. 'It gets better, young man! You're on option for *L'Uomo Vogue* and the photographer is . . . Steven-fucking-Klein!'

'And the shoot will be in New York,' adds Jo.

'Cool,' I say, finally sitting down. 'Really cool.' I've never been to New York and, no matter how much work you do as a model in Europe, New York is where the real money is. Sinatra was right. If I can make it there . . .

'We should hear about it in the next few days,' says Jo. 'Other than that, you're pretty free for the rest of the week. Not much going on straight after the shows . . . '

'Keep checking in, though,' says Sam, 'between 5 and . . . '

'Yeah,' I interrupt, getting up to leave, 'I know.'

On my way to the tube, I see I have a text message from Nathalie asking me if I'm free to meet, 'to talk'. As I stare at an empty reply screen and contemplate my response, I walk past a billboard that reads *I Shop Therefore I Am* and next to it, by the side of an overflowing rubbish bin, there's a dead pigeon with a torn Styrofoam cup in front of it. I decide to call rather than text.

'Hello?' says Nathalie, after only one ring.

'Hi Nathalie, um . . . it's me,' I manage. 'How are you?'

'Hi Alex, um, I'm good . . . yeah, very good,' she replies, sounding pleased to hear from me. 'How have you been? I've been, well, I've been worried about you. We haven't . . . we haven't spoken in a while . . . '

'I know,' I interrupt. 'That's my fault. It's just . . . the shows and everything . . . I've been really, um, busy . . . '

There's a long pause. I adjust my hair in the window of a parked Range Rover.

'So, do you want to meet?' she asks.

'Yeah, that's why I called. I'm just on my way back home. I've been, um, just, y'know . . . ' I trail off as I notice there's someone sitting in the parked Range Rover and they're staring at me. 'Um, how about we go for dinner next Saturday night?' I say, walking away from the car. 'Maybe 8-ish, at The Wolseley?'

'That would be nice . . . '

'OK then,' I say, 'I'll book a table and, um, call you.'

'OK, I . . . ' she says, trailing off.

'Bye then,' I say, after a moment.

There's another pause. I turn around and the Range Rover is no longer there.

'Bye Alex.'

66

It's the first day of August and for the third day running I'm lying on an enormous pink bed by the pool at Shoreditch House. My dad's membership, like all Every House memberships, means I can get into any House from here to New York.

This is despite the fact I'm not a member and have no intention of paying the extortionate annual fee. Here's how it works. I call up, pretending to be my dad, and make a booking with a guest list. I then turn up, sign in as one of the party, and the member never shows. It's that simple.

Today is all about East End glamour and I'm sunbathing in DSquared swimwear, adjusting my Tom Ford sunglasses while checking out one of the two Brazilian girls Jono, Patrick and Rupert invited to spend the day with us. The girl, Vanessa, is in town meeting clients before London Fashion Week. She's very tall and slim, tan, with big blue eyes and long, light brown hair. She's what Jono would describe as 'stupidly fit', and I'm getting turned on watching her sunbathe at the edge of the pool.

Meanwhile, Patrick's in the pool with Juliana, an exotic brunette with long tan legs and amazing tits; Rupert's at the bar getting in another round of pink cocktails; and Jono's on the other side of the pool talking to some older-looking women while they eat lunch.

Shoreditch House is similar to Soho House. Underwhelming food, overpriced wine, snooty foreign staff. The crowd is pretty much the same too, comprising media wankers and, inevitably given our location, City boys. The only tangible difference is the roof terrace, which happens to be the single reason I come here and also why I'm so unpopular. The other guests are all enjoying lunch on the terrace, but nobody dares get into a pool full of models. Especially the blokes. I think to myself, as I look down at my oiled abs and adjust my shorts to accommodate my semi, that the people sitting around staring at us enviously know we shouldn't be here. I dismiss my paranoia as Vanessa looks at me and smiles.

'I am going for swim,' she says assertively.

'Cool,' I answer, watching her stand and adjust her bikini bottoms, admiring her perfect figure, before she steps gracefully into the pool.

Jono comes over and sits next to me. He's wearing a white sleeveless t-shirt with *2 MANY MODELS* written in large black letters on the front.

'Hey fella,' he says, shaking my hand. 'This is alright innit?'

'Yeah man,' I say. 'So, who were you talking to over there?'

'Oh just some hot little milf, y'know how it is,' he answers. 'I reckon she's on telly or samfin'. I might bash 'er later. I've got 'er number, look.' He shows me a card and I instantly recognise the name but don't believe what I'm seeing. I lift up my sunglasses and try to focus on the women, all of whom look in their thirties, but I can't make out their faces. They're staring at us and giggling. After a moment, another woman joins them. 'That's 'er,' he says. 'Not bad, eh?'

The person he's referring to does the weather for a well-watched nightly news broadcast. She's also my dad's girlfriend, Catherine. I get up suddenly, still staring at the table, and try to get her attention.

'Sorry Jono I . . . um . . . I need the toilet . . . ' I say, starting to make my way to the bathrooms-cum-changing rooms at the other side of the pool. I deliberately take the long way around so as to walk directly in front of Catherine's table. As I pass her, I lift up my sunglasses and look at her as if to say 'Get your fucking arse in the toilets!' and she spots me and catches my drift. I walk through some glass doors into a corridor with changing rooms on my left and a sign saying *No Necking* and then stand by a changing room door, not going in. After a moment, she walks through the glass doors and I grab her arm and pull her into the changing room.

'Alexander!' she says, protesting.

'What the fuck are you doing?' I yell, closing the door.

'What do you mean? I . . . ' She looks scared and trails off.

'You know exactly what I mean. My friend, Jono, has your number. Care to explain that? Or should I just tell my dad *my* version of events?'

'Look, it i*th* difficult for me . . . ' she says, distressed, not sure which way to turn.

'Difficult? Difficult how exactly?'

'Talking to you about . . . '

I interrupt her by laughing.

'Of course it is! You're the reason my parents aren't together and, as if finding pleasure in the irony, you're now cheating on my dad!'

'I don't think that *ith* really ironic . . . ' she says, after a moment.

'Don't start with me! Look, I don't even like you, so don't fuck with me!'

I'm pointing my finger into her chest and can feel her firm implants.

'Alexander, calm down,' she says, taking my finger with her hand and then holding it to her chest so I can feel her racing heartbeat. She starts to stroke my hand. 'Calm down, OK? Can't thi*th* be our little *thecret?*' I look at her face and see she no longer looks scared. She's smiling. I look down at my hand, which is now on her left breast, and then back up at her face. 'You know,' she continues, 'after last month, your father told you not to come here . . . '

Bitch. She's got me there.

'Do you really think he'll care when I tell him about you and Jono?' I say, moving my hand away from her chest.

'You know your father will take it away from you in a heartbeat,' she says, not missing a beat and pulling my hand back to her chest. 'Look *Alex*, we were only talking,' she continues, her expression earnest, my hand still on her breast. 'He might be very good-looking but you know your father better than anyone. If I had a pound for every good-looking girl *he* talked to . . . '

'OK OK,' I interrupt. 'I get it.'

Exhausted, I walk to the sink, take off my sunglasses and splash cold water on my face, before adjusting my hair and heading back towards the door.

'You'll keep our *thecret* then?' she says, positioning herself in between me and the exit. 'Or do I need to make it worth your while? He might be good-looking, but not like you . . . ' She smiles and I notice she's got her hand in between my legs. 'After all,' she continues, removing my shorts as she gets down on her knees, 'one thing run*th* in the family, eh big boy . . . ?'

Back on the roof terrace, I notice the sun has disappeared behind a cloud but decide to keep my sunglasses on anyway.

'Hey are you leaving man?' Patrick shouts from the pool, seeing me hurriedly packing up my stuff.

'Um, yeah, but you guys can, um, stick around . . . '

Vanessa, still lying by the side of the pool, has taken off her sunglasses and is staring at me.

'What if we're asked, y'know, questions?' asks Rupert, who by now is next to my bed. He says this in a low voice and widens his eyes at the end of the sentence.

'You'll be OK . . . um . . . probably . . . ' I manage.

'Oh great, thanks man,' he mutters.

Making my way around the pool to leave, I notice Catherine is back at her table. She's telling the other women something while looking at me, and they're all giggling. As I pass the table and head for the exit, I briefly make eye contact with her.

She stares at me, for a moment, and then winks.

67

I've finally tracked down Frankie and we're in Mahiki and for some reason *Don't You Want Me* by The Human League is playing and we're talking in between sips of our cocktails – Honolulu Honey for her, Mahiki for me – when, suddenly, she stops talking, puts her hand on my mouth and smiles.

'I want you to tell me something,' she says, her expression serious.

'What?' I ask, smiling.

'Well, I was just thinking of something and . . . ' she trails off and looks away, smiling to herself.

'What? What were you thinking?' I ask, by now confused and mildly irritated.

'Did you fuck anyone while you were in Paris?' she says, staring at me.

A pause.

'Why,' I ask, laughing involuntarily. 'Would that be a problem?'

'Fuck, I don't care!' she says, a little too eagerly. She takes a sip of her drink. 'That's what I wanted to talk to you about tonight anyway . . . '

'Oh?' I say, looking around the room.

'Yeah, silly!' She touches my thigh. 'Before you went away, I thought we . . . I thought we were getting a little serious.'

I consider this for a moment, survey the room again, spot a very pretty waitress.

'I just want us to have fun, Alex,' she continues. 'I like you a lot. I mean, you're beautiful. But I'm not ready for anything serious.'

I assume from what she's telling me that she's fucking someone else and we won't be seeing much of one another any time soon. I refrain from saying this aloud. After all, I knew what to expect. It comes with the territory.

'Me neither,' I say, trying to make eye contact with the waitress. 'Hey, girls just wanna have fun . . . '

68

It's Saturday night and I'm having dinner with Nathalie. In the middle of our mains – duck confit for Nathalie, sea bass for me – she starts to cry. I look around the restaurant to see if anyone has noticed, and then across the table at Nathalie.

'What's wrong?' I ask, placing my hand on top of hers.

'Nothing, it's nothing,' she says, pulling her hand away. 'I'm just . . . it's just . . . oh it doesn't matter . . . '

A pause. The restaurant is busy tonight, and I'm mindful

of people thinking I'm the cause of the tears. I feel like I'm sweating and adjust my tie.

'Come on,' I say, 'you can tell me . . . '

'I want to be happy, Alex, with you,' she says. 'I want to be happy with you, together, like we used to be.'

'Is this what you wanted to talk about?' I ask, after a moment.

'Yes. Well, no. Yes and no really . . . oh I don't know!' She looks at me angrily, exasperated, as if expecting me to say something to make things better, to make it all go away. 'Well? Don't you want to be happy?'

'Um, of course I do.' I place my hand back on hers.

'With me?' she adds, her eyes focused squarely on mine.

Another pause.

'Um . . . '

'Alex?' she says, staring at me and gripping my hand tightly. 'Do you want to be happy, *with me?*'

'Why not?' I say. I look away and, at the table next to us, a well-dressed woman wearing glasses with red frames catches my eye and I wonder to myself if she's been listening to our conversation.

'Then come away with me,' says Nathalie, grinning.

'What?' I ask, looking at the table next to us again to see if the woman's still staring.

'I've booked two flights to Nice tomorrow. We've been talking about going away all summer and I've finally got a few days off. We can stay at my parents' place until they arrive next weekend. Remember? We went there when we first got together.' She takes a gulp of wine, awaiting my response.

'But, um, what about . . . '

'Work?' she interrupts, almost spitting out her wine. 'Alex, you don't have a real job. It's not like you need to book time off!' She laughs.

'Yeah, I guess.'

'Well you could sound enthusiastic . . . '

'I am, Nathalie, I am,' I say, trying to smile. 'It will be, um, good to get away.'

'Then it's settled, OK?'

A pause, even longer than before.

'Nathalie . . . '

'OK?' she interrupts. 'I'm talking to *you*, Alex. I don't see anybody here but you . . . '

69

We're in the departure lounge and Nathalie's showing me the new perfume she just picked up in Duty Free.

'It's nice isn't it? What do you think? Don't you think it's nice?' she says.

I smell her wrist.

'It's OK,' I say. 'A little old-fashioned . . . '

'Yeah, it's nice,' she interrupts. 'I've been meaning to get it for ages. I'm really glad we decided to go away.' She kisses me on the cheek and then starts reading her copy of *Vogue* with Sienna Miller on the cover.

I look outside through the window overlooking the runway, and notice a sign on a fence around the perimeter that reads: *Crash-gate 17.*

I wonder, for a while, whether having seventeen helps.

70

I sleep for most of the flight. After landing in Nice around 9 p.m., we catch a taxi to her parents' villa, which is in the hills surrounding the city.

Nathalie's dad owns a large construction company and he

helped design the place himself. We make our way through huge cast iron gates and up a long driveway, which is home to her dad's new orange Porsche GT3 RS and an old white Lamborghini Countach that he's restoring. Outside, there's one of those pools that spills over the side to form a waterfall. I think they're called Infinity Pools, but I'm not sure.

Inside, there's little in the way of furniture – at least, functioning furniture. There are the obligatory floor-to-ceiling windows overlooking the outside sunning space, a large aquarium in one of the lounge walls and a massive open plan kitchen and dining space. There are no televisions. Each of the three large en-suite double bedrooms has a theme: West Africa for the master, Tuscany for the double and Pop Art for the single. Nathalie's mum co-owns a gallery on Dover Street and art, which features prominently throughout the villa, comes in the form of Maurizio Cattelan sculptures and what looks like a Roy Lichtenstein original.

'Great place,' I say, as we settle in the Tuscany room.

'Isn't it?' says Nathalie, dropping her bag and kissing me softly on the cheek. 'I'm going for a shower. Wanna join me?'

'You know, I will in a second, but I'd love a beer right now and, um, some air.'

'OK, but don't be a stranger . . . '

Nathalie undresses while I get rid of the cases in the huge walk-in closet. As I make my way towards the kitchen to grab a beer, I stand in the doorway of the bathroom and watch as she steps into the shower, admiring her slim body, her slender legs and perfectly rounded breasts, the tan lines on her pert bottom still visible from a holiday here in June.

After helping myself to a Desperados from the huge fridge freezer in the kitchen, I step out onto the patio and stand by the pool, taking in tonight's humid air, the impressive views of Nice and the temptation of a summer evening viewed from a safe distance.

71

We make love later that evening in bed, aggressively, which Nathalie likes, and then we do it again, afterwards, when we go outside together for some air by the pool. The second time is softer, slower, and Nathalie tells me she loves me while I'm inside her, which I don't like. Under the moonlight, the cool air on our bodies as we hold one another tightly, we look into each other's eyes in between kissing, like we mean it. Like we used to, when we first met.

I don't see anybody here but you.

72

The next morning, I wake up alone. I get up and wander through the villa looking for Nathalie, but she's nowhere to be found. I do some press-ups and then help myself to a Coke from the fridge, catching my reflection in a full-length mirror across the room. I decide I need to top up my tan so grab a pair of Gucci sunglasses I got from the show, some lotion and my iPhone, and go outside to sunbathe naked in the mid-morning sun.

I listen to half of an album by New Young Pony Club that Nathalie recommended and then decide I don't like New Young Pony Club so look for an alternative but before I can select one, as if somehow sensing that I don't like the same music as her, she suddenly appears out of nowhere.

'Hi,' she says, peering over her sunglasses at me from the French doors. 'What are you doing?'

'Hi,' I say, lifting my sunglasses. 'Um, can you guess?'

'Very funny, Alex,' she replies, not smiling. 'I've just

been to the supermarket. Are you hungry? We've got eggs, croissants, orange juice, coffee, cigarettes . . . '

'All of the above please,' I say, turning over onto my front while selecting *I'm Not There* by Bob Dylan.

'Put some clothes on then,' she says, before disappearing inside.

We eat by the pool. Sitting opposite one another with the sun beating down, I gulp down my coffee and then light a Davidoff Light, which I've been smoking since Juliette introduced me to them in Paris. Nathalie sighs.

'So, are you glad you came?' she asks. She's wearing sunglasses and looking across the table, but I can tell she's not looking at me.

'Yeah, it's great,' I say. 'The weather's perfect . . . ' I trail off, sensing she's not listening. 'What's wrong?' I ask.

'Nothing,' she says, trying to smile. 'What do you want to do today?'

'We could just stay here,' I say. 'Get some sun . . . '

'OK,' she interrupts. 'If that's what Alex wants then that's what Alex gets . . . '

73

We spend most of the afternoon sunbathing at opposite ends of the pool. Sweating profusely by late afternoon, I join Nathalie for a swim to cool off. I swim alongside her while she's doing lengths and, when she gets to the end, I try to kiss her on the neck, which causes her to tense up.

'What's wrong?' I ask, irritated. 'You've been acting weird today . . . '

'Have I?' she interrupts, not looking at me.

'Yes,' I answer. I grab her shoulders and turn her around by the edge of the pool, kissing her on the lips, holding her waist, before moving my hands up her back to unclip her bikini top.

'Stop!' she says, which causes me to retreat. 'I mean, is that all you ever want?' She gets out of the pool and disappears inside.

74

Later, we're eating a simple dinner of bream and salad with a bottle of chilled rosé wine by the pool. We've both showered to go out and are only wearing towels.

'This is good,' I say, gesturing at my fish.

'Thanks,' says Nathalie, smiling at me.

'You know,' I say, 'about earlier . . . '

'Don't Alex,' she interrupts, shaking her head. 'It's OK, really.'

'OK,' I say, sipping my wine.

'I forgive you,' she adds.

A pause. I sip my wine again.

'What do you mean?' I say, after a moment. 'Forgive me for what?'

Nathalie stares at me.

'If you don't know, Alex, why were you going to apologise just then?' she says.

'I wasn't going to apologise!' I say, my voice rising slightly. 'I don't know why you were acting that way, in the pool earlier. I just wanted to kiss you. Oh, Nathalie, please will you forgive me? Pretty please!'

'Don't be sarcastic, Alex, it doesn't suit you.'

'Why? Because I'm not clever enough to be sarcastic? Because I'm just a stupid model?' I'm yelling now but Nathalie is calm.

'Oh here we go,' she says. 'Yes, I'm attacking you because you're a model, Alex . . . '

'I suppose that's not being sarcastic . . . ' I mutter.
Another pause.

'I'm so tired of this,' she says, sounding exhausted.

'But I didn't do anything,' I say, by now frustrated.

'Fine.'

'Fine!'

Nathalie sips her wine.

'Alex . . . ' she says, after a while.

'Yes?' I say, glancing up and realising she's looking straight at me.

'Do you love me?'

'Um, of course . . . ' I say.

'Then why can't you look at me when you say it?'

'What do you mean?' I say, now looking at her.

'When we made love, last night, I told you I loved you and you didn't say anything. You just looked at me. You used to tell me you loved me all the time.'

'Is that what this is all about?' I ask, gesturing towards the pool.

'What do you mean?'

'Coming away together. Is that what this is all about?'

'I thought we needed to spend some time together . . . '

'Face it, Nathalie,' I interrupt, 'we can't go back to the way we were.'

'What? I don't . . . why not?'

'Because we were in a bubble back then, when we met. It's not real life. We were at university, barely even turning up to lectures, and we just wanted to have fun. And we did. We did have fun together but . . . things are different now.' I sigh and down the rest of my wine. 'We can't . . . we can't go back to all that.'

'I don't want to go back to anything. I want to be with you, now, and I want you to love me. Is that too much to ask? Or is there not enough of you to go around anymore?'

'What do you mean by that exactly?' I ask, watching her as she stares at the pool.

'I know about you and that girl Frankie,' she says, still staring off into the distance.

'What do you mean, me and . . . '

'Don't start with me, Alex!' she interrupts, slamming her hand down on the table and staring at me. 'Do not lie to me. I know you've been seeing her. Rebecca told me . . . '

'What does that bitch know about anything?' I yell, thinking to myself that I didn't even realise Rebecca knew Frankie. 'She's coked up half of the time and the rest she's being fucked by some rent boy.'

'She was fucking Hugo, last time I checked,' she says, smirking.

I stand up, walk over to the pool and light a cigarette. Nathalie follows a moment later and stands next to me. She touches me on the arm.

'Are you denying it?' she asks. I can feel her looking at me but I'm just staring off into the distance, at something, anything, as long as it's far away from here.

'Yes, I'm denying it,' I say, after a moment, still not looking at her.

'Tell me now,' she says, grabbing my arm and turning me to face her. 'Promise me that you've not been seeing Frankie.'

'Um . . . ' I look down at my feet.

'Thank you,' she says. 'That's all I needed to hear.' She starts to walk away but I grab her arm, turning her to face me.

'Do you want me to stop seeing her? Is that what you want? I will you know, if that's what you want . . . '

'I don't care, Alex,' she says softly, after a moment. I can see tears in her eyes but she's not looking at me and is trying not to cry. 'I know you've not always been faithful . . . '

'Wait . . . ' I interrupt.

'No, don't,' she says, holding her hand to my mouth. 'I

don't want you to lie to me. Not again. I know we've not always got on. But I . . . I thought we had something . . . '

'We did, I mean . . . we do,' I say.

'You were right the first time, Alex,' she says. 'We did have something, once. We *were* in love, past tense.' She walks away towards the villa.

'Wait,' I say, grabbing her arm again to stop her. 'You know, you've not always been faithful . . . '

She turns around to face me and stares at me angrily.

'You're going to throw that back in my face, after what you did to me that night? I find out you were fucking Katie, my best friend, and your best friend's girlfriend, and you think you can be mad at me for . . . for kissing another boy, when I was drunk, when I was upset? You should be glad I never told Hugo . . . '

'OK, OK,' I say, turning back to face the pool. 'I'm just saying neither of us is perfect . . . '

'I've never claimed to be perfect,' she interrupts, grabbing my arm and turning me to face her. She's crying now. 'But I've always loved you and I still love you, despite everything, and I'm telling you, right now, that if you *can't* tell me you love me then . . . then, it's over.'

I look at her and in a flash I think of when we first met, in a greasy spoon café just off the Strand. We both studied English Literature and had missed the very first lecture of the course because it was at 9 a.m. and we were hungover from the night before. We'd both turned up fifteen minutes late and ended up in a café across the road from university, getting over our hangovers with mugs of builders' tea. We only found out we'd both skipped the same lecture after half an hour of talking, and we laughed. We always laughed together. When we were leaving the café, I slipped something I'd just written on a napkin while she was in the ladies into her notebook. We were inseparable from that moment.

'You know what your problem is, Alex?' says Nathalie, backing away from me. She's stopped crying and is staring straight at me. 'You don't know how to love.' She turns away and walks back towards the villa. This time, I don't stop her.

I sit here, thinking, in this dark and cold café, that I will love you, anytime.

And I know I'll love you, anytime.

75

We get up early the next morning and Nathalie borrows her dad's Porsche to drive me to the airport. The only thing she's said so far today, over breakfast this morning, is that she's going to stay in Nice and have some time to herself before her parents arrive on Friday.

'So, um . . . ' I say as we pull up to the terminal, not sure where I'm going with that sentence but wanting to say something, anything, to break the silence.

'Have a safe flight,' says Nathalie, after a moment, a pair of white wayfarer sunglasses not quite concealing the tears in her eyes.

'Nathalie . . . I . . . '

'Yes, Alex?' she says, looking at me. A tear runs down her cheek.

'I . . . I think . . . ' I look away and out of the window at Arrivals, which is situated on the ground floor next to where we're parked, and I watch people pushing trolleys full of suitcases, excited-looking children holding onto parents, families starting a holiday, something new and a break from, well, something else. I lean over to kiss Nathalie, but she pulls back.

'Bye Alex,' she says, gripping the steering wheel tightly and looking straight ahead.

'Bye Nathalie.'

I get out of the car and it skids as Nathalie drives away, rejoining the main road and speeding off into the distance.

76

I walk into Departures and call Veronique in Paris.

'Salut . . . um, c'est Alex, ça va?' I manage.

'Alexander, 'ello!' says Veronique. 'I'm very well, 'ow are you?'

'Um, I'm OK. I'm in Nice. I've just been on, um, holiday, and I wondered if there was anything for me in Paris . . . whether I should stay in the country, y'know . . .'

'Why but of course! Where are you now?'

'At Nice airport.'

'I will call Jo and then call you back. We will see if we can get you on a flight to Paris this morning, OK?'

'OK.'

As I sit in a café, waiting for Veronique to call me back, I think of Nathalie and for some reason picture the first love letter she ever gave to me. She'd written it during a lecture on some scrap paper. It was the first time she'd said 'I love you' but, as I sit here now, not touching my espresso, I think instead of the words she'd used at the end of the letter.

I don't want things to ever change.

77

I manage to get on a flight to Paris later that morning. As soon as I land, I go straight to my agency.

'Salut Alexander!' says Veronique, standing up from her desk to kiss me. 'Welcome back to Paris.' She's always friendly and each time I come to Paris, for whatever reason, I can't complain. She's an affable old lady who treats me well, but I know that if I wasn't getting so much work – and if she wasn't making nearly seventy per cent on every job – she would soon resemble most other Parisians her age. C'est la vie.

'Hi, um, I hope this is all OK . . . ' I say while her little dog jumps up at me.

'But of course, you are welcome any time,' she smiles. 'Jo told me about, ah, Kate Moss and said to me that you are on option for *L'Uomo Vogue* also. That is fantastique, but it is not until next week so you can be 'ere until then. There are, 'ow you say, lots and lots of castings. I 'ave one for you this afternoon. Yohji Yamamoto is casting for 'is look book. Tomorrow, editorials. You can get more pictures maybe this week also.'

'So I'll be busy then,' I say, removing a pile of superfluous cushions from a large leather chair and sitting down. 'Can I leave my case here for now?'

'Of course,' she says, walking over to the printer in the corner of the room. Framed copies of *Vogue*, *Elle*, *10* and other fashion magazines, with models from this agency on the covers, decorate the wall above her head. There's even one of me, for *l'Officiel Hommes*, leaning back against a wall wearing a tuxedo and cummerbund, no shirt. One hand is behind my head and I'm staring, head tilted slightly to the right, as if to say 'I've been expecting you'. 'Do you have your book?' she asks, walking back over to me.

'Of course,' I say, getting up and pulling her chair out for her. 'Where will I be staying?'

'Merci,' she says, sitting down. 'I have a very nice room for you, with another model, in Opéra.' She hands me a piece of paper with today's casting details and I start to walk out of the room.

'Who will I be staying with?' I ask, standing in the doorway.

'Bailey,' she says, staring at her screen. 'You 'ave met

before I think. Well, you are both 'ere for one week together. C'est bon, non?'

78

On the way to my casting for Yohji Yamamoto, I buy a seven-day travelcard and have to get my picture taken in a photo booth at the station because I lost my pass during the shows. After fifteen minutes waiting by the machine for the photos to appear, I'm disappointed to find I look really tired, the ink accentuating dark circles under my eyes. I resolve to get another done next time I'm in Paris, when I'm not so stressed.

The casting is in a small studio in a pretty courtyard, just off Avenue de la République. There are no other models and I think to myself that I've not seen one since arriving in Paris. Inside the studio, I'm greeted by a small Japanese man dressed all in white. He introduces himself as Ari or something like that, shakes my hand and takes my book.

'Did you, ah, do the show?' he asks, flicking through my book.

'In Fashion Week?' I ask, confused, before realising how stupid I sound. 'Of course that's what you meant, um . . . ' I trail off as he just nods, almost solemnly. 'No, um, I didn't.' They usually go for weird-looking guys and I'm starting to wonder why I've been sent to this casting but then I notice he's looking at a photo of me in my underwear and seems interested.

'This is, ah, berry nice,' he says, after a while. 'What for?'

'That? Oh, it was for Calvin Klein, in Milan. It was the first time I'd done a shoot in my underwear, and there was this girl, also on the shoot, and we had to get quite, um, raunchy and . . . ' I trail off as I realise he's just nodding and staring at the photo and not listening to me at all.

79

After going back to the agency to pick up my case, I make my way to the hotel in Opéra and am relieved to find that Bailey's not in the room.

I dump my case in the hall and take a look around, which doesn't take long. The room has two beds and a tiny shower room and, after two minutes, I'm dreading the thought of spending a week here with Bailey.

I stretch out on one of the beds and decide to call Juliette, hoping to see her, maybe stay with her, but she doesn't answer her phone so I leave her a message.

'Salut Juliette! C'est Alex, ça va? OK, well that's about it for my French but, um . . . ' I start to feel tense, get up and walk over towards the open window, look out onto the street below. There's an argument going on between a taxi driver and some builders and *La poésie est dans la rue* is written in large red letters above a patisserie near to where they stand. 'So,' I continue, 'I'm in Paris and I've come to rescue you from your evil boyfriend and teach you some more about English boys. I'm only here for one week so, um, don't miss out, OK? Call me.'

After I hang up, I immediately regret the message and wonder whether I can delete it. Realising that this is a ridiculous idea, I go for a long shower instead.

In the shower, I let the hot spray hit me in the face for what feels like half an hour, trying to wake me up. I wash my body with some lotion enriched with jojoba oil and, even though my abs feel hard and cubed, I start to wonder whether I need to go to the gym soon to put on a bit more bulk.

Stepping out of the shower, I stand in front of the mirror and decide that my body looks good after all. In fact, it looks better than just good. My shoulders, arms and chest are well-defined, my abs like the proverbial washboard and the lines above my hips more pronounced than ever. Turning around, my back is smooth and muscular, demarcated by a prominent line leading down to my posterior, which most girls say is the best part of my body. That and my face, of course.

Looking closer in the mirror, though, I see that my complexion is flushed. I'm convinced it's because I'm tired so I apply a cream containing grapeseed oil to reduce puffiness and then some Clinique Daily Eye Hydrator to diminish the appearance of fine lines and shadows.

I step back into the room, still nude, and see I have a new voicemail. It's from Juliette.

'Salut Alex, ça va? This is Juliette, I 'ope you guess this already!' she laughs. 'I am, ah, 'appy to 'ear you 'ave visited again, so soon. Why not you come to meet me? I am, ah, on Rue de l'Ecole de Médecine. Yes, I am a famous doctor one day! You will see. Take the Metro to Odéon and call when you are 'ere, OK?'

80

I meet Juliette outside a café across from Odéon station, which is near her college. It's the archetypal Parisian place with round tables and wicker chairs and she's sitting in front of a large open window, looking more beautiful than I remember. It's cool in Paris today but she's wearing a strapless white dress and sandals, her slender legs crossed underneath the table. She embraces me warmly as I get to the table and invites me to sit on the other half of her large chair so we're side by side, looking out onto the busy streets of Saint-Germain.

'Hi,' I say, after a moment during which I look at her peripherally, while she looks ahead, admiring her almost overpowering beauty and affected manner. She's holding an unlit cigarette between her lips, looking through her Balenciaga bag for a lighter, and her hair is down and it looks messy, but in a good way. Her full lips look moist but she's not wearing lipstick. In fact, I don't think she's wearing any make-up. Her complexion is so impossibly smooth, however, as to suggest she is. I don't mind this pretension of effortlessness, even of innocence. In fact, it turns me on.

'Bonjour,' she says, removing the cigarette and smiling at me before biting her bottom lip, involuntarily, I think. I continue looking into her deep brown eyes and only break my stare when a waiter passes. I order an espresso and look back at Juliette. She's still rummaging through her bag and I notice the cigarette that is between her lips again has somehow broken, but she doesn't realise and this makes me smile. She finds a lighter and then offers me a cigarette.

'I'll take this one,' I say, taking the broken one from her lips. 'You're not cool enough to pull that off . . . ' I laugh and she thumps me gently on the arm and smiles, blushing slightly. 'How are you?' I ask, lighting what's left of the cigarette and making a mental note to pick up more Davidoff Lights while I'm in town.

'Very 'appy,' she says.

'You're happy to see me?' I ask, smiling.

'Why of course! But I am 'appy for other reasons too . . . '

'And what might they be?'

'I, ah, don't understand . . . ' she says, frowning and then pouting in a very cute way.

'I mean, *why* are you happy?'

'Oh, I do not know,' she says, laughing. 'I 'ave just started at my college and I love it . . . '

'You're going to be a famous doctor, *non*?' I interrupt, laughing.

'But of course,' she says, her manner serious. 'I am to be a plastic surgeon!'

I laugh loudly and she hits me softly on the shoulder again, this time leaving her hand there.

'I'm joking,' I say. 'I'm very happy for you. Perhaps you can help me to look beautiful when I'm old and ugly!'

'That will be, ah, très difficile I think!' she says, nodding and laughing loudly.

'Thanks!' I say, laughing. She smiles at me.

'So . . . ' I continue, moving closer and turning to face her, 'how is your boyfriend? Have you decided you prefer English boys?'

'That is why I am very 'appy, Alex,' she says, taking her hand off my shoulder. 'We are, 'ow you say . . . ah, yes . . . we are engaged.'

A pause.

'But . . . ' I say, trailing off. 'I thought, um, he . . . '

'I know, I know,' she interrupts. 'But we are in love, and when we talked, well, I know we are in love. Arnaud, my boyfriend, told me 'e loved me and only wanted to be with me, forever. Look at my ring.' She holds out her hand to show me but I don't really notice the ring and just smile.

'That's great,' I say, looking away and out of the window.

'Are you 'appy for me?' she says.

'Do you want the truth?' I say, inhaling a long drag of the cigarette.

'Of course! I want us to be friends and we must 'ave the truth to be friends, *non*?' I look at her face and she looks radiant, staring at me earnestly and awaiting my reply.

'Yes, we must have the truth, to be friends. That's important . . . ' I say, looking away again.

'So,' she says, after a moment, 'are you 'appy for me?'

'Yes, it's wonderful news,' I say, kissing her softly on the cheek. 'I am very happy for you.'

81

I eat dinner in a small restaurant in Saint-Germain, alone, before drowning my sorrows in a bar near my hotel. At around midnight, tired and slightly drunk, I reluctantly make my way back to the hotel. Bailey is lying on his bed, wearing only underwear, when I enter the room.

'Well, look what the cat dragged in,' he says, smiling at me.

'Hey, um, how are you?' I say, sitting down on my bed, which is no more than a few feet away from his.

'I'm very good,' he says, changing the channel on the television a couple of times before eventually settling on German MTV. A video by Tears For Fears is on but I can't remember the name of the song.

'So, um, how long are you in town for?' I ask, after a while. I glance over at him, his muscular legs slightly apart, and I can't help but notice an impressive bulge in the white briefs.

'Oh, just for the week. I'm on option for something in New York next week, and I need to be home anyway because school's starting. I've got my final year to finish.' I look back at the television and a man is singing to a librarian while checking out a huge pile of books. 'How long are you in town for?' he asks, turning on the bed to look at me. Even though he's on his side, I can still make out his well-defined stomach muscles and I start to wonder to myself whether his abs are better than mine.

'The same. I have an option too, in New York as a matter of fact. Small world, right?'

'Is it for *L'Uomo Vogue* with Steven Klein?' he asks, staring at me.

'Um, yeah . . . I think so, um, I can't remember . . . you know how it is . . . ' Great, I think to myself. That's just great.

We both watch television from our beds for the next half an hour or so, in silence, before he turns back to face me.

'Can I ask you a question?' he says, his expression serious.

'Sure,' I say. 'What do you want to know?'

'Why did you turn me down, in Paris?' A video by Pet Shop Boys comes on at that exact moment and I laugh out loud. 'What's so fucking funny man?' he says, still looking at me.

'Nothing,' I say, looking back at him. 'I'm sorry.'

'So, why did you turn me down?' he asks, after a few minutes.

'Because I'm not gay!' I say, by now irritated. I look back at the television. A new video is on and a man, dressed as a cowboy, is standing in a desert with his back to the camera. He turns around and fires an imaginary pistol.

'Neither am I, man,' he says, after a while. 'Fuck, this is the twenty-first century. That shit doesn't matter . . . '

'OK OK, I get you. What I mean is, I'm not really, um, into that, y'know . . . '

'Into what?' he interrupts. 'Taking it in the ass?'

'Well . . . *yeah!*' I say, looking at him again. My voice is much louder now. 'I'm not into that.'

'That's not what I've heard,' he says, smiling to himself and looking back at the television.

'What's that supposed to mean?' I ask, staring at him.

'I've just heard otherwise,' he says smugly. 'That's all I'm saying . . . '

'Who have you been talking to?' I interrupt.

'It doesn't matter,' he says. 'Forget I mentioned it.'

'Tell me!' I yell, sitting up on the bed and staring at him angrily.

'You know Francesca Balfour, right? She's a fashion student, in London, very hot . . . '

I look at the television screen.

I will deliver you know I'm a forgiver.

Reach out and touch faith.

Reach out and touch faith.

'Um, yeah, I know her . . . ' I say, after a moment.

'Well, I've been seeing her again recently,' he says, sitting up on the bed so he's facing me. 'I met her during London Fashion Week, and I was in town again after the shows last month. I came to Paris from there only yesterday actually. Anyway, I've been seeing her and she told me she knows you and that you and her had a thing, a lifetime ago, and, I don't know how or why this came up, but she told me you liked it in the ass. Don't worry about it. I mean, I do too. It doesn't make you gay or anything . . . '

'I can't believe I'm hearing this,' I say, interrupting him. 'Look, I don't know what Frankie's told you but, um, we've never been together and I, um, am not into that, OK? And it's not because I'm against gay people or anything like that. Hey, I'm open-minded but . . . look, I just didn't want to do anything, in Paris, OK?'

'OK man,' he says, lying back on the bed. 'Whatever you say . . . '

82

Mercifully, my agency faxed through a test shoot last night at midnight so I don't have to spend time with Bailey today. I get up early, while he's still asleep, and sneak out.

The shoot starts at 8 a.m. so I grab a pain au chocolat from a boulangerie near my hotel and jump on the Metro. An hour later, after changing twice and feeling nauseated on the RER, I finally arrive at a small warehouse in a gloomy eastern suburb.

The photographer is some big time Indian guy called Raj or something like that and he does all the major editorial shoots in town apparently. He's not at the warehouse when I arrive, though. In fact, nobody is. I stand outside a huge door and buzz all four buttons until a girl, who I'm sure has nothing to do with the shoot, opens the door in her pyjamas. My French is not up to it but she guesses why I'm here and, after what I think is a flurry of swear words aimed in my general direction, lets me in before disappearing back upstairs.

The studio is on the ground floor. I bang on the door for a moment and, confusingly, a small man with a bleached blonde crew cut and sunglasses who looks like a photographer lets me in. I don't ask why he didn't answer the buzzer or even whether he is a photographer and instead just sit down on a huge white leather sofa.

On one side of the room is a tiny kitchenette and on the other, which is unfurnished, is a large white board propped up against a wall. The space has a high ceiling, and when I look above the kitchenette area I see a small ladder leading up to where the blonde man presumably sleeps. It looks tiny and barely big enough to sleep in, so calling it a bedroom would be pure hyperbole.

'Would you like a coffee?' the man asks in an American accent. He's in the kitchenette, not facing me.

'Sure, thank you,' I answer, flicking through a copy of *Vogue* with an oh-so-obviously-photo-shopped picture of Kate Moss on the cover. 'Are you, um, taking part today?'

'No,' he answers, presenting me with a small cup of what looks like black sludge. 'You'll just be using my space.'

'Oh, OK . . . um, do you know when everyone is getting here?'

'I think soon . . . yes, soon . . . ' he says, nodding but clearly puzzled. He walks away again and starts cleaning his tiny kitchenette, wiping the work surfaces, washing up a glass and a plate, and he's starting to freak me out and I wish he'd just stay still.

After half an hour of reading fashion magazines – or, to be more accurate, looking at the hot girls in the innumerable ads – other people finally begin to arrive. A small blonde woman who looks like a stylist is followed in by an even smaller Japanese man who looks like a make-up artist. Immediately after that, a tall girl walks through the door with an Indian man who's wearing a black bandana and silver Rayban Aviators.

'Alex, right?' the Indian man says, setting down a large bag on the sofa next to me before shaking my hand. 'How are you?' His accent eludes me but sounds more English than anything else.

'Yeah, um, I'm good, thanks,' I say, standing to attention. The tall girl sits down on the sofa and doesn't say a word.

'Have you been here long?' he asks, walking over to the large white board and inspecting it.

'No, um, not really,' I say, still standing.

'OK, so meet Julia and Bebo,' he says, gesturing to the blonde and the Japanese man who both seem to be just following him around, not talking. I wave and smile.

'I'm Alice,' says the tall girl, from behind.

'Oh, hi,' I say, sitting down on the sofa next to her.

'We're doing an editorial today with Alice,' the Indian man yells from across the room. 'But she'll take ages getting ready – y'know, hair and make-up *etcetera* – so we can get you done before lunch. Sound good?'

'Sounds great man,' I yell back.

While everyone sets up and generally fusses around, I take the opportunity to get to know Alice. She's tall and very thin, with long blonde hair, and is, well, odd-looking. Her eyes are wide apart, her nose slightly retrousse, and her lips look swollen. She's not unattractive, but she's definitely odd-looking.

'So, what brings you to Paris?' she asks, leaning back on the sofa so her tight T-shirt rides up, revealing a flat, tan stomach. I assume you're not here full-time. I would've noticed you . . . '

'I live in London,' I say, relaxing back on the sofa to match her pretension of indifference. 'I'm here until the end of the week, just doing castings, getting some more pictures, meeting clients. You know how it is . . . '

'Sure,' she says. 'Excuse me,' she shouts to the Japanese man, 'can I get a glass of water or something?' He nods and shuffles off, returning a moment later with a glass of water. She takes a sip and pulls a disgusted face before setting the water down and never touching it again.

'How about you? Are you based here full-time?' I ask, after a moment.

'Yeah, um, I'm from Surrey, originally, but I've been here for two years now. It's OK, I suppose. I mean, I love Paris, but my agency really fucks me off, y'know, because they take all my money and still complain about my weight. Apparently, I'm not as thin as I used to be.' She gestures incredulously and rolls her eyes. 'Anyway, what was I saying? Oh yeah, well, I miss home, y'know, family and friends, and I think I'll go back for Christmas and stay there. You never know . . . '

'I love Paris too,' I say. 'I mean, it's such a romantic place. I know that's a cliché but, um, it is!' I laugh and Alice smiles. 'But I'm only here for a week and have to stay in a room with a complete dickhead. It's just, well, it's too much.' She's nodding. 'He thinks he's an "It Boy" or something,' I continue. 'He's so into himself. He just annoys me, I guess. Anyway . . . ' I sigh.

'You know, I have my own apartment. My agency got fed up of girls moving out when they had to live with me, so they just stuck me on my own. I live in Oberkampf. If you don't mind mess, you could stay with me. I mean, if you want to . . . '

I'm so happy and relieved that I almost throw myself at her in gratitude.

'That would be amazing!' I say. 'I mean, um, if you don't mind . . . '

'No worries. I'll be here all day by the looks of things, but if you give me a call later you can come over with your stuff and, well, move in I guess.' She takes her book out of a large red Mulberry bag, removes a card and writes down her number. 'There you go,' she says, handing me the card. 'Oh yay! We're going to be roomies!' She claps her hands and grins.

'Cool . . . ' I say, smiling.

83

I leave the shoot at noon and spend most of the day wandering around Notre Dame and the Left Bank, taking photos of the sights on my iPhone. Tourists are everywhere. There's this one American family – parents, both wearing baseball caps and bum bags, and two young blonde boys – and the kids are running around outside the cathedral and swinging on the lamp posts and they go round and round and round and I take a photo and immediately think that people are watching me.

When I get back to the hotel, Bailey's in the shower. I try to gather my things without him noticing me but, as I make my way to the door with my case, he walks out of the bathroom and confronts me in the doorway.

'Hey,' he says, drying his short wet hair with a small towel, a larger one wrapped around his twenty-nine-inch waist. 'What's up?'

'Hey,' I say, 'um, well, I met a girl today, at a shoot and, um, I'm going to stay with her, y'know . . . '

He frowns and looks disappointed, but then just brushes past me.

'Whatever,' he says, standing by his bed, not facing me. 'Well, if you want to meet up for a beer or anything, you have my number . . . ' I start to walk out of the room. 'And Alex,' he continues. I turn around in the doorway. He's still not facing me. 'You know where I am, if you want anything . . . ' he says, dropping his towel on the floor.

84

I spend the rest of the week hanging out with Alice going to a few castings but mostly following her around while she goes to hers and we have fun together and she shows me hidden areas of the city where there are no tourists and I tell her 'I'd like to stay if I could speak the language' and she says 'You could always learn and stay with me' and by the time I leave we're like old friends.

85

I arrive back in London on Sunday afternoon. When I get home, I'm surprised to find Andreas is still not in the flat and I'm sure some of his stuff is missing. I only notice this when I'm about to take a shower. I ran out of shampoo weeks ago and have been borrowing his Aveda Pure-Formance cleanser, but when I go into his bedroom it's not where I left it, and some of his stuff – clothes that were on his floor, a laptop that was on his desk – is missing. It almost looks like someone's broken into the flat and removed a few items at random.

I forget about it and walk into the bathroom. Looking in the mirror, I decide I look like shit so I shower and use some Lab Series Multi Action Face Wash to reinvigorate my skin. I step out of the shower and moisturise before applying some Lab Series Instant Moisture Eye Gel to revive tired, stressed-looking eyes and then a Lab Series Purifying Mask, which uses activated charcoal to extract impurities and unclog pores.

I settle down in front of the television and, after flicking channels for an hour, get up to pick out one of Andreas's DVDs. They're all missing too, so I go back to the sofa and end up falling asleep in front of a reality show with troubled celebrities I don't recognise competing for a place in rehab.

86

First thing the next morning, I go to my agency to check in and tell them about Andreas.

'Hello stranger,' says Jo as I walk into men's division. She kisses me on both cheeks and then stares at me, inspecting my face. 'You look tired, young man. You really need to start looking after yourself more. I have lots of requests for you this week and you're going to be really busy. London Fashion Week's next week but if you go to castings looking like this, well, you'll put us out of business . . . '

'Yeah, I know,' I say. 'I've just been, um, a bit stressed and, well, the travelling and everything . . . I'll be fine . . . thanks for the, um, concern . . . '

'*Anyway*, we've got good news,' says Sam, interrupting. She's appeared out of nowhere and is standing next to me. 'We just had a call from Veronique in Paris and . . . you've got the Yves Saint-fucking-Laurent campaign!' She's grinning and hugs me before I can say anything.

'Wow that's great!' I say, pushing her away. 'How much . . . '

'And Steven Klein is still on option,' Jo interrupts. She's now sitting down, her headset on. 'There's been a delay because apparently he's shooting Hayden Christensen for his new movie and, well, we're just waiting for the details. It's going to happen babes, don't worry.'

'Yeah, so, fingers crossed,' says Sam, smiling and crossing her fingers. I just stare at her and she sits back down at her desk.

'Look, can I, um, ask a question?' I say, sitting down on an empty seat between them. 'Have you spoken to Andreas? I got home last night and, well, he's still not there and I thought he was only staying in Milan for a few weeks and it looks like some of his stuff is missing and . . . '

'Slow down, Alex,' says Sam, interrupting me again. 'Andreas came back to London last week, while you were away. He's going to stay in Milan, for the time being. The market's better there for his look, so you won't be seeing him for a while.'

'He looked really thin, didn't he?' says Jo, still staring at her screen before looking up at Sam as if to suggest she shouldn't have said that. 'He needs to start looking after himself,' she continues, looking at me. 'Like another young man I won't mention . . . ' She flashes a fake smile at me, glances at Sam, and then goes back to her screen.

'We'll move some other boy in with you soon so don't worry,' says Sam dismissively. 'We're refreshing our board and letting go of a few people but for the time being at least you'll have the place to yourself, so make sure you keep it tidy.' Sam puts on her headset and stares at her screen, which is my cue to leave.

87

I've already had three request castings this morning for editorials in *Arena Homme +* and *i-D* and *AnOtherMan* and I'm now on my way to one for a *GQ Style* editorial feature they're calling 'Britain's Next Top Male Models' and all this afternoon I have castings for London Fashion Week and I'm pretty tired but slept all day yesterday and so I think I look OK.

I arrive at Vogue House and sign in and after being given a security pass and told to go to the third floor by an unfriendly receptionist who looks like Amy Winehouse before all the drugs, I take the lift with a couple of boys I recognise, maybe from London, maybe from shows in Paris and Milan, but I don't speak to any of them and instead watch a show from Milan Fashion Week on Fashion TV, which is on in the lift, and I try to spot myself but only manage to catch a glimpse of Bailey.

Upstairs, a few other boys are waiting in a small reception room. After ten or fifteen minutes of just standing around, a group of boys are called in and, only moments later, they file out one by one, climb into the lift and disappear.

When it's my turn, a young girl with very short bleached blonde hair wearing a Siouxsie and The Banshees T-shirt, drainpipe jeans with turn-ups and Dr. Martens leads me though a large open plan office and into a small room. An oldish man with greying hair and black sunglasses is sitting behind a desk and he tells me to sit down. After flicking through my book and picking out three cards, he takes off his sunglasses and looks straight at me.

'You did the Gucci show, didn't you?' he says, staring at me. 'I was there . . . '

'Yeah, um, and some other shows. I've just got the Yves Saint . . . '

'I know you've got that campaign,' he interrupts, laughing. 'That's why you're here.'

'Ah, I see,' I say, fidgeting in my chair. It's cold and I wonder to myself why they need to have the air conditioning on all the time in these places.

'Look, I'm sure your agency told you but we're doing a feature for the next issue on British boys, on the ones who are going to be big next year. You're one of those boys.'

'Um, OK,' I say. I'm about to ask why I needed to come in

but he laughs and holds up his hand, preventing me from speaking.

'I suppose you're wondering why you've had to come in, right? Well, things are going to change for you from now on, trust me. I've been in this business a long time and I know that when a boy like you gets practically every show in a season, things are going to change. I just wanted to check you out in the flesh. I see you've got great skin. That's a big plus. Do you look after yourself? Be honest . . . '

'Yeah I do, but, um, I've always had good skin, I guess . . . '

'Take off your shirt for me and stand against that wall behind you.'

I take off my shirt, thinking to myself that my tan looks good in this light, and stand against the bare and expansive surface. He gets up from his chair, grabs a camera and takes a few Polaroids.

'Great, you look great,' he says, going back to sit down. 'So, the shoot will be next week, the day before Fashion Week starts. I understand, from your agency, that you'll be doing some shows . . . '

'Yeah, um, I'm not sure. I've got some castings . . . '

'Alexander, remember I just said things are going to change for you? You won't be going to castings like before. Your face is on everyone's list. You'll have requests, you'll turn up and show them you actually exist, and that's it. Make no mistake, things are going to change.'

88

I have a request casting for an über trendy designer on Denmark Street and I know him so don't have to wait around or anything which is cool.

'Hey,' I say, popping my head around the door and smiling at Marco, the designer, who's sitting behind his desk in the far corner. I've met him loads of times, mainly because he frequents most of the fashionable bars around town and has a penchant for male models, whether they're actually modelling or, as is the case with most of them, waiting tables.

'Look who it is, everyone!' he says, clapping his hands and smirking. 'We've heard all about you in Paris and Milan. Is there anyone you didn't do?'

'Not literally, of course!' says Christian. Christian is Marco's graphic designer or something like that and he's sitting on the other side of the room, laughing hysterically at his own joke.

'Nobody wants to hear what you have to say,' says Marco, flashing a catty smile at Christian. 'Give us your book then.'

I hand him my book and sit down on the corner of his desk, thinking to myself that I need to make sure my agency get prints of all the recent stuff I've done.

'You know our show is going to be just girls, right?' he says, flicking through my book. 'Well, I'd still like you to be in it. Agyness is opening and she's huge this year so . . . '

'Just like you Mister!' Christian interrupts, still laughing.

'I said shut up you queen!' Marco yells, throwing a pencil at Christian. He smiles at me. '*Anyway*, we'd like you to end the show together.' He holds up his hands as if framing something in the empty space between us. 'Best of British! That's the theme of the collection.' He looks away and hands my book back to me.

'OK, cool,' I say, picking up an over-sized purple T-shirt with the words *I'M NOT A T-SHIRT* printed in large yellow letters on the front, 'but I don't have to wear one of these ridiculous T-shirts, do I?' I duck as he throws a pencil at me.

'Wait one second,' he says as I approach the door, his phone ringing. Christian is waving V-signs and smirking at me from his desk by the door. 'Can you hold for a second, please?' I hear Marco say. 'The show is on the last day of Fashion Week and we've got a party afterwards so I expect to see you there. *Hello*! I'm talking to you . . . '

'Yeah of course,' I say, looking back at him and winking. 'I'm DTF if you are . . . '

89

I did the shoot for *GQ Style* yesterday and we were all dressed in Paul Smith and later when I told Jo she said 'He wants you for the campaign and maybe the fragrance but don't get excited – yet!' and that's really cool because I've heard the money is amazing.

90

I've just left a fitting for the Tristan Thorne show at London College of Fashion and need to be back there in a few hours for another fitting so go to a café nearby even though I've already had three coffees today and really just want to go home.

I sit down by the window and call Hugo. I've been trying to get in touch with him for weeks now and want to know if he's up for going to some parties, but he's not returning my calls or answering my e-mails and I even poked him on Facebook but he didn't poke me back. I call his mobile and it rings and rings but he doesn't answer, so I try him at work.

'Hugo speaking,' he answers, after only one ring.

'Hugo, hi . . . it's, um, Alex,' I manage.

'Alexander, um . . . look, I'm a bit busy right now, can I call . . . '

'I've been trying to call you for a week, Hugo,' I interrupt, my voice quivering. 'What's up? I, um, wondered whether you wanted to go to any, um, shows or parties, y'know . . . '

'I don't think so, Alexander,' he says, after a moment.

'Hugo?'

'Yes Alexander . . . '

'What the fuck is wrong with you?' I say, my voice louder now. 'You've not returned my calls and now you're just being weird . . . '

'I haven't got time for this,' he interrupts, his voice flat and calm. 'I'll call you.' He hangs up.

91

London Fashion Week has been a blast and I've already done shows for Gareth Pugh and MAN and Peter Jensen and it's been cool but tiring because I have to wait my turn while the girls get hair and make-up done and this takes a long time but just proves how the girls are in charge in this business and because London Fashion Week is mostly for girls and isn't about menswear there are hardly any other boys here and I have to share toilets that are covered in diarrhoea what with the laxatives and all.

I've been to parties thrown by Eley Kishimoto and Paul Smith and Sam Taylor-Wood and I've met Anouck Lepère who's cute and Lily Donaldson who's also cute and I was on a table in Sketch with Freja Beha and Hilary Rhoda and Jamie Dornan and Iekeliene Stange and Julia Dunstall and in Cuckoo I sipped Cosmopolitans with Lily Cole who's nice but too serious and I laughed at something Daisy Lowe said to Greg Krelenstein on a crowded dance floor in Crystal and at some point at the launch of a hot new swimwear label called Bisou I talked for a long time to some guy called François-Henri Pinault who was hanging around Giancarlo Giammetti and at a party in Shoreditch I saw Jamie Hince and Jefferson Hack talking to one another but Kate Moss wasn't there which was disappointing.

On Wednesday I went to Met Bar with some models from the Gareth Pugh show and it was packed and there was one boy who I think did Galliano with me and he was wearing a strap-on cock on his head and a girl was posing with him and licking the strap-on for the photographers and a crew from FTV were also there and someone from behind the camera shouted 'Do models eat?' while I was helping myself to hors d'oeuvres and I just shrugged and later I met Giorgio Armani and the lead singer of Maroon 5 tried to talk to me about global warming but I was busy talking to the DJ whose name is Elixir but that's not his real name and I know him from when he used to model but he's not modelling anymore and I think he's a writer but he likes to adopt different personas become different people and right now he's a DJ with a penchant for electro-pop and military uniforms and red lipstick and later he let me share the decks with Jodie Harsh and actually spin a record and I chose *Chant No. 1 (I Don't Need This Pressure On)* by Spandau Ballet and the crowd loved it.

And then there was last night when I went to the Paul Smith party and I was asked if I wanted to meet him and I said 'Sure' as if I wasn't bothered but really I was and I sat at his table and he poured me a glass of champagne himself and then I talked to an American girl who I think does the campaign for La Perla because she looked familiar and her body was amazing and we did some coke in the toilets and she showed me how to do it using one of her Parliament cigarettes because the filter has a recess and we both laughed at being such a cliché and I was too drunk to remember to ask for her number but I don't think it really matters because the girls never go out with the boys anyway.

This brings me to tonight and I'm doing Marco's show to

close Fashion Week but I only have one look comprising a pair of purple briefs with Marco's face on the crotch and a cropped hoodie with *DON'T BE A CO2NT* written on the front so I don't show up until around half an hour before it starts.

While putting on Marco's ridiculous briefs I'm introduced to Agyness Deyn and she's very Northern and tells me her real name is Laura or Lauren or something really plain-Jane like that and I think to myself as we make small talk that she looks prettier in person than in pictures and there are these tiny bottles of champagne being passed around before the show and despite the fact I don't like Moët I'm quite drunk by the time she opens.

The MisShapes are playing live and it feels like a long time before all the other girls have done their thing but after Marco grabs my arm and snatches me away from a girl I'm talking to who's getting undressed I realise it's my turn and with the lights flashing and the music blaring I walk out holding hands with Agyness and at the end of the catwalk she leans in to kiss me and then pushes me away and watching as she skips back up the catwalk I just shrug to the hundreds of lenses trying to capture the essence of what we're all doing here.

Everyone is happy backstage and we all toast Marco and he thanks us one by one even me and then we all go to Punk for the after-party and I'm on a table with Marco and Christian and Agyness and we're all drinking Mojitos topped with rosé champagne and they all laugh when I say I thought Marco fancied me when we first met and he says 'You wish!' and when I'm queuing for the toilets I bump into Jo and she hugs me and says 'You were great today babes' and she tells me to come by the agency because the shot of Agyness pushing me away at the end of the catwalk is going to be in tomorrow's *thelondonpaper* and I wonder to myself how she can possibly know this.

At some point I do some shots of I don't know what at the bar with some androgynous looking girls from the show and they ask me what my fantasy is and I say 'Doing coke off a supermodel's arse-crack' and they all laugh thinking I'm joking and maybe I am because by the time it gets to 2 a.m. I'm honestly too drunk to see straight and so I leave the club to get some fresh air and then it all gets a bit blurred and I think I end up jumping into a cab home because when I wake up the following afternoon I'm fully clothed on my sofa and I can't remember how I got here.

92

'Babes!' Jo yells as I walk into men's division the next day, still a little worse for wear. 'You look great. I'm jealous.'

'Yeah, I wish I could party like you and still look good,' says Sam, grinning. 'In fact, why don't you just fuck off?' They both laugh hysterically.

'I'll be back in a second,' I say, dropping my new Missoni bag that I bought just to carry my book in by Jo's chair and heading towards the bathroom.

Looking at my reflection in the mirror, I wonder how they came to the conclusion that I look good today. I splash some water on my face and feel better, before heading back towards men's division.

Passing Guy's office, I notice he's at his desk and a skinny young girl with long red hair and freckles is sitting across from him. I hover in the corridor for some reason, thinking to myself that I recognise her. She looks upset but he's just staring at her and she bursts into tears and he says flatly 'Babes we can only send you to castings but once you're there it's down to you' and when he sees me looking he winks.

They're only after your money.

I head back to men's and sit down next to Jo.

'So, what have you got for me?' I say, smiling.

'One second, I'll get you up on my screen . . . ' says Jo, staring at her screen intently and scrolling through dozens of names and faces that all blur into one until she gets to me. 'Have a look at this while you're here.' She pushes a copy of yesterday's *thelondonpaper* across the desk.

I look at the picture of Agyness Deyn pushing me away. The headline reads: *Looking This Good? A Push Over!*

'OK,' says Jo, 'so we're still waiting for details on YSL but we think it will be two shoots and it will definitely be last minute so be prepared. Steven Klein is happening in the week before Christmas so it will be in time for the shows . . . '

'Wait, Steven Klein is confirmed?' I ask incredulously. 'Why didn't you say?'

'Not confirmed yet, young man,' she says, laughing. 'It's on option but it *will* happen. Now, the shoot will be in New York and they'll fly you out before the shows. You can meet your new agency and then fly to Milan with the American boys. I think that makes the most sense . . . '

'OK, so I have a New York agent now too?' I say, laughing. 'But I didn't even see any . . . '

'Of course you have an agent there!' says Sam, butting in. 'Steven-fucking-Klein baby! You're going to be huge next season.'

'Talking of huge,' says Jo, 'you're on option for Paul Smith. I'm just waiting on that but it looks good. I can't tell you how much it is because it'll get your hopes up but . . . '

'It's mega!' Sam interrupts. 'You're going to take us all out aren't you, once you're rich?'

'Um, of course . . . '

'We've still got to decide what to do with you, after YSL,' says Jo.

'What do you mean?' I ask.

'Well, there are some editorials. The *Numero* cover for

135

one. But we need to see how it goes here, because if Paul Smith confirm . . . '

'*When* Paul Smith confirm . . . ' Sam interrupts, again.

'Yes, *when* they confirm, you're going to be busy doing stuff for that so, well, watch this space.'

As I get up to leave, the young girl from earlier storms past me and out of the room, slamming the door behind her.

'Another one bites the dust,' says Sam, raising her eyebrows.

'I told women's she wasn't right,' says Jo. 'She just didn't have enough . . . '

'Personality?' Sam says, laughing.

'Exactly,' says Jo, her expression serious. 'I'd say it's about ninety per cent personality, ten per cent looks. Wouldn't you Sam?'

'Oh yeah, absolutely . . . ' says Sam, giggling to herself.

93

I'm lying on my sofa in front of the television, still trying to get over the other night and also waiting to hear back from Hugo. I left him a message at work earlier when he didn't pick up, which is not like him, and I was pretty angry in the message but I think he'll call me back.

I'm watching a programme on Kate Moss that looks at her success as a model while charting the changes in society over her career. During the ads, I get up to grab some pomegranate juice from the fridge and check my phone, which is recharging in the kitchen. No messages. I go back to the sofa and an advert for a beauty company comes on. It shows a montage of women and all these body hang-ups about feeling fat, ugly or not blonde enough appear on the screen next to the sad faces, and it's all to the sound of someone singing *True Colours* and at the end it just says *Normal is Beautiful*.

It's raining outside. I stare over at the open window for what feels like a long time, but don't get up to close it.

94

Jo wasn't exaggerating when she said 'be prepared' because she's just called to say that the first shoot for YSL is tomorrow in Cannes and they're flying me out first class tonight.

I'm still packing when right on schedule I get a call that a silver Toyota Prius is waiting and after deliberating over whether it will still be hot in the South of France and then deciding which shoes to pack I make my way outside and the driver offers to take my bag but it's a brand new Louis Vuitton Nomade Keepall that cost £1,790 so I put it on the backseat with me instead.

It takes a long time to get across town to Heathrow and this is made worse by the fact I have to pretend to listen to the driver droning on about the congestion charge and how it's only succeeded in reducing traffic but not congestion which is different apparently.

When we do finally arrive at the airport with only moments to spare I check in and see I'm flying BA and am relieved and I get through security without a hassle and after ordering a stale muffin in Starbucks that I don't finish and flicking through a copy of the latest *L'Uomo Vogue* in the first class lounge it's time to board and I smile at a grumpy-looking woman checking boarding passes and she's oldish maybe forty and she smiles and this makes me feel good and so I sleep contented for most of the flight.

Another car this time a Mercedes and not a hybrid picks

me up at Nice airport and drives me to Cannes which is
farther away than I realised and still tired despite resting on
the plane I sleep for most of the journey before arriving at the
Majestic Barrière on La Croisette and checking into my room
which is huge and my itinerary says I have breakfast with the
photographer at 8 a.m. so after a protracted and ultimately
fruitless attempt to find German MTV on my television I take
a quick shower and go to bed.

95

I'm eating a breakfast of Eggs Benedict and fresh fruit while
pretending to listen to the photographer's 'vision' for today's
shoot. I didn't catch his name but I think he's Japanese, and
he's not eating but looks like he needs to. He's very skinny and
this is made worse by his choice of attire: a New York Yankees
baseball cap, worn back-to-front, of course; a huge white
FUBU T-shirt; baggy jeans; and a pair of box fresh Nike Air
Jordans. I can barely understand a word but I'm nodding and
smiling at his two assistants, who also look Japanese and just
sit there giggling.

As I finish my breakfast, a tall man with grey hair and
black sunglasses sits down at our table.

'Alexander, my name is Laurent,' he says in a thick French
accent, holding out his hand. 'I am, ah, very pleased to meet
you in person.'

'Hey,' I say, shaking his hand. 'And you are here
because . . . ?'

'I am, 'ow you say, the creative director for Yves Saint-
Laurent . . . '

'Any relation?' I interrupt, smiling.

'I, ah, do not understand . . . ' he says, confused.

'A joke,' I say, smiling at the girls. 'Sorry . . . ' I make a funny face as if to say 'Oops!' and then wink at them, which makes them giggle and then, after a moment, Laurent laughs really loudly like it's the funniest thing he's ever heard.

96

It's hot in Cannes but not as hot as I expected and the shoot takes place on a yacht and the whole idea is 'luxury without effort' according to Laurent and I wear all white a white jacket white shirt white trousers white shoes and the yacht's supposed to be mine and apparently I just lounge around on it all summer relaxing and saying 'Welcome aboard!' to someone anyone the audience I suppose and we take all day and the two Japanese girls just help me in and out of clothes and alter my lapel or collar or sunglasses or whatever and Laurent interferes constantly and keeps reminding us all of the 'essence of the brand' but it's worth it because I'm shown Polaroids and the lighting is really flattering and I look tan and like I could actually own this yacht which is ridiculous given that I've already spent most of the money from the campaign in advance and can barely afford my outfit right now but it is I suppose what they're going for.

97

In the shower later, I shampoo and condition my hair with a hybrid cleanser containing seaweed, sage extract, spearmint oil and liquorice, and use an organic exfoliating wash on my body. Stepping out while still wet, I spray what's left of my re-energising serum on my hair, before combing it back carefully off my face. I dry myself with a towel and then moisturise my body in front of a full-length mirror, making sure I properly apply the body butter, which is enriched with coconut oil and Vitamin E to my chest, stomach and genitals. I dab my face with a warm flannel and shave, before splashing cold water on my face and dabbing it again, this time with a fresh hand towel to close the pores. I then apply an oil-free moisturiser, taking care to avoid my eyes, and study my face in the mirror – high cheekbones, full lips, flawless complexion – before wrapping myself in a towel and leaving the bathroom.

I've managed to find German MTV on my television and put it on in the background while deciding what to wear for dinner. As I'm carefully laying out my outfit on the bed, there's a knock at the door.

'We are waiting for you . . . ' says Laurent, smiling awkwardly as he notices I'm only wearing a towel.

'Sorry, I didn't realise,' I say apologetically, but he just shrugs as if he doesn't really care.

After slipping into a pair of Calvin Klein briefs, some J. Lindeberg skinny jeans, a shirt and waistcoat by 7 For All Mankind and a pair of new Paul Smith brogues, I take another look at my reflection in the huge mirror in my room and think to myself that this is the first time I've ever looked like something out of one of my shoots.

98

I'm with Laurent and the photographer and the two Japanese girls and we're having dinner at l'Annex and Laurent and the photographer are droning on about the shoot the brand the future for the company and the two girls just sit together giggling.

The photographer makes his excuses and goes back to the hotel after dinner because apparently he's got a headache but I heard him on the phone earlier and he sounded like he was arranging to meet someone but I couldn't really tell and so the rest of us go to Bâoli and we end up on a table in the club and Laurent seems to know everyone in Cannes and stands by the bar talking to the owner and we're served drinks all night without having to order any.

The DJ's playing *Happy Dreamer* by Laid Back and it's really loud and on the other side of the club in a small booth I spot two boys I recognise from Paris and tired of sitting with one boring Frenchman and two giggling Japanese girls I go over to them and Julien who did the John Galliano show with me and Luc who opened for Sonia Rykiel both recognise me instantly *I'm a happy dreamer* and they tell me to sit down and help myself to a magnum of Veuve Clicquot *I'm a happy dreamer* and I notice they're with a girl *I'm a happy dreamer* and she's very pretty but also very young *I believe in love* and she looks drunk and I smile at her and she smiles back *I believe in you and me.*

'OK man I see you like 'er well she is a friend of Julien's and goes to school in Cannes and wants to be a model' Luc explains in the toilets later while he and I wash our hands and then he starts fidgeting with his tie because he's so wired and says 'Alex don't worry my friend' while turning to face me and grabbing my shoulder 'I think she is 'ow you say up for it!'

99

Later, the four of us are waiting for a cab to go to Julien's hotel room but it's taking a long time because Bâoli is not in the centre of town. It's quite cold now so I wander around the car park to keep warm, before making my way over to the marina nearby.

Standing on some rocks, looking out to sea at yachts that look like twinkling stars in the night sky, I light a cigarette and think about the last few weeks, reflect on everything that's happened, everything that's going to happen.

Make no mistake, things are going to change.

100

I sleep for most of the next day because it was such a late one last night and my flight back to London is not until 7 p.m. but I end up sleeping for most of the car journey to the airport anyway and after almost missing my flight because I'm so tired I actually drop off in the departure lounge I sleep until just moments before we land and I think I'm having a nightmare about Julien and Luc and the girl until Laurent squeezes my thigh a little too hard and says 'Are you OK?' and I realise where I am but don't know the answer to his question.

101

I'm in a club on Brick Lane, trying to get served while thinking of how I'll spend the money when I get the Paul Smith campaign. As the barmaid passes me over in favour of a grubby-looking student, I look beyond her and stare at my reflection in a mirror behind the bar. Smiling without candour as I survey the room, and temporarily giving up on my pursuit of alcohol, I see a group of people I went to university with at the end of the bar. One of them, a tall, skinny boy called Tell, holds up his digital camera and says 'OK, smile, and everybody say "cash" '.

I turn back to the bar, stare at my reflection again. Two

young-looking boys – one tall and blonde, the other not as tall and not as blonde – come to stand next to me.

'Do you like Miss Black America?' the tall boy asks the other boy while staring at me.

'Um . . . the TV show?' says the other boy, utterly perplexed.

'No, the band.'

'Not really . . . do you?'

'No. Not really.'

I go to the gents. The room is bathed in red lighting and, in the cubicle opposite where I stand, there's a mirror with *I told you I was hardcore* written on it in permanent marker.

On my way back to the bar, a blonde girl with a red ribbon in her hair smiles at me and I smile back. I recognise her from the group earlier. I think I've met her before, possibly at a casting, and her name might be Ana or Anja but I can't remember. She's good-looking with blue eyes and full red lips and long brown hair and as I get closer I notice she has a small tattoo below her belly button.

Fast getaway here.

'Hi Alex, you having fun?' she says, offering me a white pill as I push through crowds of people and move towards the bar.

'Absolutely!' I reply, waving my hand to turn down her offer because I haven't got a drink and don't want a bitter aftertaste.

'This is just like when Starlight opened!' she exclaims. 'Did I see you there? Anyway . . . what was I saying?'

I laugh and, grabbing a cocktail napkin from the bar, write the words *BEER PLEASE* and wave it at the barmaid, and I'm convinced by now she's a lesbian because she looks straight through me.

'Oh yeah, Starlight . . . so I was proper pissed and there was free champagne and Charlie for VIPs and there was this guy and I was like "I'm not that kind of girl" but I went back to his anyway and we didn't *do* anything. I'm not that kind of girl.'

As I realise I'll end up sleeping with this girl tonight, I recall a conversation I had with Hugo, back at university, when we first met. It was the first year, during freshers' week, and we were sprawled on my bed in my room late at night, smoking joints, which was something we did a lot that year.

'I've never told anyone about this, Alexander, but I became infatuated with a boy I grew up with,' he told me. He paused to take a drag on the joint, before passing it to me and getting up to walk across the room. He changed the song on the CD player to *A Groovy Kind of Love* by Phil Collins, which made me laugh. 'We once broke into a derelict industrial building,' he continued, standing by the sink in the corner and looking at his reflection in the mirror. 'We smashed the windows and old office equipment with crowbars we found inside, and then we played around with the fire extinguishers. Why am I telling you this? Oh yeah. He was, I think, my first romantic ex-perience. I can still remember the adrenaline and the tingle in my dick . . . ' He trailed off and smiled to himself, nodding, as if remembering a joke he didn't want to tell, and then came back to lie on the bed. I thought to myself, as he reclined next to me, that he looked handsome. 'Anyway,' he continued, looking at me, 'my point is that I would say he's the reason for my current view on sexuality.'

'And what's that?' I asked, passing him the joint.

'The only thing that matters is the result.'

I leave the girl's flat while she's still asleep. During sex her smile was soft and sanguine.

I still can't remember her name.

102

I'm on my way to a request casting for *Dazed* and as I step off the train and make my way out of the station I see a *No Begging* sign that looks exactly like a *No Smoking* sign and on the escalators there are video screens showing an ad for Agent Provocateur that says *Understand Me Seduce Me Buy Me* and when I finally reach the surface outside on the street I pass a busker playing Schubert's *Ave Maria* on an out-of-tune violin while a beggar sits sullenly next to a rubbish bin and there's a middle-aged woman holding a can of cider and posing outside an All Saints and she's standing perfectly still like a Covent Garden statue performer.

La poésie est dans la rue.

103

Later, I'm standing in a long queue in Abercrombie & Fitch, returning some T-shirts, when someone tugs at my arm. I turn around and it's Rebecca.

'Alex?' she says, her expression suggesting she's incredibly surprised to see me. 'I thought it was you! I've been queuing behind you for, like, ten minutes and I thought to myself "That's Alex" but you look, um, *different* . . . and I didn't have the courage to say anything! How stupid is that?'

'Um, very stupid?' I say, about to turn back around before changing my mind. 'What do you mean, different?' I ask.

'Oh, just, y'know, *different*,' she says, shrugging. 'You look great, though. I saw you in the paper, y'know, and I was *sooo* jealous! Agyness Deyn is, like, my idol!' She's stroking my arm and I consider removing her hand but then reconsider as I notice, glancing at her chest, she's not wearing a bra.

'Look, do you wanna go out for dinner with me?' I say, after a moment. 'Or are you busy?' I let out a short laugh at the end to accentuate my confident approach.

'Yeah! I mean, yes, I'd love to get something to eat with you, I mean, that would be, um, nice . . . ' she says, blushing.

104

Later, at Beach Blanket Babylon Shoreditch, I'm listening to Rebecca drone on about her non-stop partying and rampant drug use and how she's always wanted to come to 'the three Bs' and I'd normally be getting bored at this point but instead I'm nodding happily while topping up her wine.

As she gets drunker and drunker, I only want her more and more. I'm getting an erection at the thought of her naked and I think she knows, despite being inebriated, that she's turning me on. She keeps loosening her blouse and flashing cleavage, biting her lip, and as she gets drunker this flirtation just gets more and more overt and I find myself laughing at various points, but she just thinks I'm enjoying her tedious story and continues flirting.

When the bill's presented – £50 a head not including wine and definitely not worth it – she stops her story and looks at me, her expression very serious.

'Alex,' she says, her fingers toying seductively with the stem of her now empty wine glass. 'Can I ask you a question?'

'Sure,' I say. 'What do you want to know?' I smile at a hot-looking waitress as she takes payment and then saunters away.

'Are you seeing Nathalie or not? Because I've heard from Hugo that you're not and . . . ' She trails off, awaiting my response.

'Did Hugo tell you that? I mean, while you two were seeing each other . . . ' I say, slouching back in my seat.

'I've not been seeing Hugo,' she says, confused.

'You've not?' I say, also confused. 'Then when . . . how . . . did Hugo tell you this?'

'Well, he didn't, but I bumped into him and Nathalie in Bungalow 8 and I just wondered, because you weren't there . . . '

'When was this?' I interrupt, sitting up and looking around the room, panicking, as if I think I'll spot them here together.

'Oh I don't know, maybe last week. So you're not with her then?'

A pause while I consider this, decide whether I believe her, whether I care.

'Does it look like I'm with her?' I say casually.

'And you're OK with them spending time together?' she asks, after a moment.

'Why wouldn't I be?' I say, shrugging. 'Whatever.' I stand up and put on my jacket, before walking over to her and kissing her hard on the mouth. 'Ready?'

105

I wake up the next day to find my bed empty and Rebecca gone. When I get up to wander into the kitchen, though, I see her standing there, naked, buttering some toast. As she stands side on, unaware of my presence, I study her petite body, the s-curve of her arched back and rounded arse, the worked-out physique of someone who spends a lot of time in the gym, firming up.

'Morning handsome,' she says, turning to face me while taking a bite of her toast. 'Want some?' She rolls her shoulders back and pushes out her chest, and I stare at her rounded breasts – fake, but very nice – and smile.

'Sure, why not?'

You don't know how to love.

The only thing that matters is the result.

106

I'm walking down Poland Street on the way to my agency and it's only 4 p.m. but it's already getting dark and I can't believe it's nearly winter.

I make my way upstairs and in reception, reading a tattered copy of Marx's *Economic and Philosophic Manuscripts of 1844*, I spot Patrick. I go over to sit next to him but, from the expression on his face when he looks up at me, I don't think he wants me to.

'Hey man,' I say, slumping on the sofa next to him. 'So, how you been?'

'Um, not bad,' he says, glancing at me before looking away.

'What are you waiting for?' I ask, after a moment. 'I mean, in here . . . '

'Oh, um, I've got to see Sam about something,' he says, still not looking at me. 'I don't know, um, I think I owe a lot so, y'know . . . ' He trails off.

Patrick did Gucci in Milan but he's been doing this for a few years now and his career hasn't really taken off. He's been to Paris and Milan countless times but rarely gets work, so his account is perennially in the red. He doesn't have to pay a penny unless he works, of course, but sooner or later something's got to give.

'Have a look at this,' he says, turning to face me and handing me a piece of A4 paper. It's his statement. According to this, he owes just under £1,000 for a couple of return flights to the shows, one test shoot, numerous prints and laser copies for his book, mail outs of his portfolio, head sheets, cards and CDs, not to mention dozens of charges for postage and couriers, all in the space of six months. During that time, not counting the Gucci show in Milan that his agency out there collected on, he hasn't worked once.

'Wow . . . ' I manage, after a moment. I look at the coffee table in front of us and notice a copy of *GQ Style* with me on the cover. I'm with four other boys dressed in sharply-tailored Paul Smith suits and we each have an outline drawn around us as if we're something you can cut out and keep. I stare at the magazine and will it to turn over or disappear somehow.

'Hey man, don't worry about me,' he says, taking the statement off me and trying to sound upbeat. 'I think I'll go back to university. I never really gave it a chance the first time so . . . yeah . . . I think I'll do that . . . '

107

The money from the shows, half of which I've already spent in advance, has just cleared in my account. Keen to celebrate and determined to make up with Hugo, I head over to his new apartment. He never did give me the address but I still have the magazine he showed me, so know where it is. They can only have one penthouse, I assume.

When I arrive at the riverside apartment complex, however, I realise my plan has a flaw. There's an elaborate entry-phone system and, of course, I don't know his apartment number. I give him a call on his mobile, on the off chance he's forgotten why we're no longer speaking, and he actually answers.

'Alexander, what's up?' he says, his voice flat and calm as ever.

'Um, Hugo, hi . . . it's, um, me . . . I know you know that already . . . um, can I come up? I'm outside . . . '

'You're outside now?' he interrupts, no longer sounding calm.

'Yeah, um, is that OK?'

A pause. It's growing darker and starting to rain.

'OK,' he says. 'I'm in Building Two, number 101.'

I spend what feels like a long time finding the right entrance and lift but eventually arrive on the top floor of Building Two. I walk out of the lift and see another lift in front of me with a buzzer next to it. I press it and wait.

'Alexander?' says Hugo, through the speaker.

'Yeah . . . '

There's a beep and I hear the lift moving. After a few seconds, the doors open and I step inside. When the doors open again, after a moment, I'm in Hugo's apartment.

'Come in and sit down,' he shouts from the other side of the room. He's wearing a pink Ralph Lauren shirt and some denim shorts and is lying on a huge sofa in what looks like the lounge, surrounded by floor-to-ceiling windows overlooking the Thames. It reminds me of his office.

'This is, um, really nice, Hugo . . . ' I say. 'Aren't you going to, um, show me around?' He's watching television and not looking at me. Sensing he's not keen, I sit down on the sofa opposite him.

A long pause while I watch him watching.

'So, what brings you here, Alexander?' he says, sitting up suddenly and switching off the television.

'Um, well, I guess I, um, wondered what was happening, with you, and whether you and I were, y'know, cool . . . '

'Why wouldn't we be *cool*?' he says, staring at me, his expression serious.

'Hugo, what is this?' I say, after a moment. 'You've got me here thinking I'm in a job interview or something . . . '

'Don't you mean a casting?' he interrupts, his expression still serious.

'Look, whatever. I came here because we haven't spoken in ages and I thought you might want to, y'know . . . I mean, why *haven't* you been returning my calls?'

'I've been busy,' he says. He stares at me and just shrugs.

'OK, I get it. This was a mistake. I thought you'd want to, I don't know, talk or something, but clearly you don't.' I get up and start to walk back towards the lift.

'Wait,' he says, getting up and walking over to where I stand in the hallway. I turn around to face him and notice, hanging above an ornate dressing table next to us, a large kind of abstract painting of a girl and I think I recognise her but can't be sure. He stands facing me but doesn't say anything.

'OK, so I'm waiting . . . ' I say, after a moment.

'Why did you really come here, Alexander?' he says.

A pause.

'I, um, don't know. I guess I just wanted to talk to you . . . '

'I don't believe you,' he interrupts, walking towards me. 'I think you're here because you want something.'

'What do you mean?' I ask, confused.

'You want something that you can't have.' His expression is almost aggressive and, given the fact that he spends his spare time playing rugby and I spend mine, well, enjoying the finer things in life, I'm starting to get a little worried.

'OK, so what's that supposed to mean? Don't start talking in riddles, Hugo. Next it'll be fucking Latin . . . '

He pushes me, hard, and I stagger backwards towards the lift.

'Alexander, don't start with me!' he says, his voice loud now. He walks towards me so he's in my face again. 'You know why we're here so why don't you just come out and say it?'

'Um . . . ' I manage.

'Fucking say it!' he yells, grabbing hold of me by my shirt.

'Get off me!' I shout, shoving him backwards. 'Look, just calm fucking down, OK? I've not come here for a fight . . . '

'OK OK . . . ' he says, staring at the ground.

'I really don't know what you mean, OK?' I say, after a moment.

'Why are you here, Alexander? Think about it.'

'Nathalie?' I venture, after another moment.

'What's Nathalie got to do with anything?' he says, looking genuinely puzzled. 'You're here because of Katie . . . '

'Wait, Katie?' I say, interrupting him. 'Why would I be here because of Katie?'

'Because of . . . ' he trails off.

'Because of . . . what?' I say.

'Fucking hell, you don't know,' he says. His voice is quieter now but he has an intense expression on his face. 'You really don't know do you?'

'No, clearly I do not fucking know about Katie!' I yell. 'What do I need to know about Katie?'

He walks back into the lounge and I follow him, grabbing him on the shoulder and turning him around to face me.

'What has Katie got to do with anything?' I ask.

'Alexander, I know, OK?' he says, not looking at me.

A pause. I step backwards involuntarily.

'You know . . . um . . . what?' I say.

'Don't make me say it, Alexander . . . ' he says, trailing off.

I know exactly what he's going to say but, for some reason, I don't leave the apartment. Instead, I just stand there, frozen.

'I came here because of Nathalie,' I say. 'I've heard, um, that she's been seeing someone . . . '

'And why would that be a problem?' he says, looking straight at me.

I look again at the painting next to us and think it looks like Nathalie.

'I heard she was seeing . . . you,' I say, gritting my teeth.

'OK, that's great,' he says, smiling.

'Are you denying it?' I ask, confused by his response.

'No I'm not denying it. We've seen each other a lot recently but nothing's happened. We're not together. Do you think I'd do that to you? I'm not like you, Alexander. She needed someone, when she came back to London, after you left her in France . . . '

'Wait, go back a second,' I say, interrupting. 'What do you mean, not like me?'

'Do you really want me to say it?' he says, staring at me, his fists clenched.

I look at him, at how angry he is, and realise what he's getting at.

'Look,' I say, after a moment, 'me and Katie we . . . we were never together or anything . . . it was just once when, um, we were drunk . . . '

'Well you must be really good then,' he says, laughing.

A pause.

'What do you mean?' I ask.

'Are you telling me you only slept together one time?' he says, grinning.

'Yes, Hugo. I promise you, we were only together once, and it was a mistake. I'm sorry, OK? Forgive me, please . . . '

'It's too late for that, Alexander. And really, you shouldn't be asking *me* to forgive you.'

Another pause.

'I don't understand . . . '

'Look,' he interrupts, 'you don't know what I thought you knew, when you came here, OK? I can't say it. I can't bear to say it and look you in the eye.'

'What the fuck are you talking about?' I say, utterly perplexed. 'I don't understand . . . '

Before I can finish, he grabs me and shoves me towards the lift, pressing the button so the doors open and then pushing me inside.

'Talk to Katie,' he says, and the doors close.

108

It's dark by the time I leave Hugo's and, still a little shaken, I jump into a cab.

'Where to fella?' the driver asks.

'Hammersmith, please,' I say, after a moment. 'Vixens. Do you know where it . . . '

'Yeah I know where it is, mate,' he interrupts, laughing. 'Don't you worry . . . '

109

As soon as we get to Vixens, I head straight to the bar and casually look around the room. I don't spot Katie and think to myself that maybe I should just leave but, after noticing a significant improvement in, well, *quality* since my last visit, I decide to stick around.

I down six or seven beers and drop countless pound coins into the ubiquitous parade of pint pots while watching the dancers and standing at the front, by the stage, and soon I'm quite drunk and almost forget that I've come to see Katie. Pulling myself together as yet another girl walks off stage, gathering her clothes from the floor, I decide I need to find her, if only to find out what Hugo was going on about, so I head to the private room at the back because, let's face it, she's going to be there if she's anywhere.

As I enter, an oldish man brushes past me and I notice a girl getting dressed at the back. She's naked and is very thin with disproportionately large breasts that are round and firm-looking. She's pretty, maybe Russian, with long blonde hair, and is the only person in the room other than me. I stand in the doorway, wondering what to do, until she looks up at me.

'A dance is twenty pounds but you must wait,' she says. 'I am on break now.'

'Um, OK . . . ' I say, walking towards her, 'but . . . um, well, I'm actually looking for someone . . . '

'Who?' she asks. She's now wearing very slutty lingerie and is zipping up what looks like a uniform for a waitress in an American diner.

'Um, her name is Katie . . . ' I say, trailing off as I wonder whether she ever uses her real name here.

'I not know Katie,' she says, looking away.

'OK she's, um, slim with dark brown hair. She's pretty and, um, English . . . ' I trail off and she just stares at me. 'Oh, I know!' I say, suddenly remembering something I wish I couldn't. 'She has a tattoo on her, um, next to her . . . ' I point at my crotch.

'OK!' she says, laughing. 'I know. But I am not, ah, supposed to talk to clients about other girls . . . '

'Is she working tonight?' I ask, moving closer to her.

'No, I am sorry,' she says. The girl walks past me but then, in the doorway, turns around. 'I will tell you when she is working if you buy a dance.' She smiles at me seductively.

'No thanks,' I say, walking towards the doorway to leave. 'I'll just come back . . . '

'Wait,' she says, blocking me in the doorway. She's not zipped the uniform up to the top and I stare at her ample cleavage. 'What if she is not working for long time?'

'Then I'll keep coming back . . . '

'One dance,' she says, interrupting me, 'and I will give you her, ah, mobile.'

'Is that allowed?' I ask, smiling.

'She told me, ah, a handsome boy would look for her but there is no handsome boys come in here,' she says, smiling. 'Until now . . . '

110

I'm in Paris doing the second shoot for YSL today and we're shooting in a suite in Hôtel Costes and I've only been here for half an hour and I'm standing with my back to the camera in front of a topless girl who has long flame-red hair and full red lips and bright blue eyes and we're looking for 'One iconic shot!' according to the South African photographer who's really annoying and keeps calling me 'bru' and telling me to lift my face closer to the girl so he can see my profile and telling the girl to pull me closer to her and saying 'Look beyond the lens baby!' but after maybe half an hour he says 'We got it people!' and we wrap in time for lunch.

I thought it sounded like a lot when Jo first told me about the money until I spent half of it on a Jacob watch that's on order and asked her over breakfast at The Wolseley the other day how much the girl will be getting for doing exactly the same as me only wearing women's clothing and Jo told me 'Add a zero hun!' and laughed hysterically and I almost choked on my French toast but hey it's only money.

As I sit eating lunch with the girl I think to myself that it's been weeks since I talked to Hugo and I've not called Katie yet because I'm not really sure what to expect and up until three months ago I hadn't seen her in over a year and we'd kept it that way for a reason and yes we'd slept together while I was going out with Nathalie and she was with Hugo and yes I'd enjoyed it and yes I'd developed something like feelings for her and was hurt when she dropped off the face of the earth but that doesn't mean I want to see her now or to find out what Hugo meant when he said 'You really don't know do you?' because if I'm honest I'm not sure I care.

111

I'm asleep on my sofa when my phone rings. It's Patrick.

'Hey,' I say, glancing at my watch that's just arrived. It has a black dial with a white mother of pearl centre, four distinctly coloured time zones – Paris, New York, L.A. and Tokyo – as well as the main dial in the centre, and it's presented on an alligator skin strap. 'It's nearly midnight, Patrick. What's up?'

'What are you doing right now?' he says, sounding a lot happier than the last time I saw him.

'Um, I'm not sure,' I say. 'I'm pretty tired because I had a shoot yesterday in Paris and, um . . . why?'

'Look man, Rupert's in Camden so Jono and I are going to meet him now but then later we're all going to the Holloway Road for a house party. It's fancy dress – ironic romance or something fucking lame – but that doesn't matter. We're all going to wear suits and look like yuppie bastards. Credit crunch chic, man!' He's laughing and I can hear something going on in the background. 'Alex, are you still there?'

'Yeah, I'm not sure . . . '

'Come on!' he interrupts. 'Celebrate my freedom with me! I'll text you the address and afterwards . . . well, we're all going back to Rupert's, OK? We'll have guests, if you know what I mean . . . ' He laughs again.

'OK,' I say, knowing exactly what he means. 'I'm on my way.'

112

It takes a long time to get across town and, by the time I arrive at the party, I'm no longer in the mood.

'Alex!' Patrick yells as I walk through the open front door of a huge town house, which looks in desperate need of repair and like it's probably occupied by squatters.

'Hey man . . . ' I answer, struggling to hear myself over the music because it's so loud. 'Where can I get a drink to catch up?'

'Here you go, fella!' says Jono, suddenly appearing from behind Patrick and handing me a plastic cup of something red.

'Come with me!' says Patrick excitedly. 'I want to introduce you to some people . . . '

We make our way upstairs, past beautiful young girls and boys dancing half naked around a DJ who's completely naked, clapping his hands above his head and playing *Teen Age Riot* by Sonic Youth, before entering a large room that only has mattresses and deckchairs for furniture. Rupert is standing in between two girls. One's blonde and the other brunette, but they both look very young, maybe underage, and are obviously very drunk.

'Why don't we get out of here and have some real fun?' says Patrick, grinning. 'Who's with me?'

Before I can say anything Rupert high fives him.

'Count me in! What do you say fella?' says Jono, looking at me and grabbing my shoulder.

'I've just got here,' I reply, removing his hand. 'You can't have been here long . . . '

'Trust me, Alex, you're not missing anything,' says Patrick, taking me by the arm and escorting me out of the room.

113

After standing on the main road for fifteen minutes and despite the protestations of the driver, all six of us eventually pile into a cab back to Rupert's place.

I'm squeezed in between Patrick and Jono on the back seat. To my left, perched on Patrick's lap, the blonde girl is chewing gum and looks bored, but when our eyes meet she smiles and I notice for the first time that she's really pretty. The brunette, to my right on Jono's lap, is kissing him and this prompts the blonde girl to start kissing Patrick while Rupert, who's sitting across from us, just stares.

We crawl through traffic for what feels like a long time before finally arriving at a mansion block somewhere in Covent Garden. Rupert's parents bought an apartment for when he moves to London after university, but he seems to spend a lot of time in it now and I'm not sure he's even going back to university.

Rupert apologises for the state of the place as we enter the living room and assures us he's not really moved in. It looks pretty impressive to me, though. The room is vast and there's a huge flat-screen television on one wall above an enormous fireplace and two large sofas, the only furniture in the room, are positioned in front of it.

As I walk over to one of the sofas with the blonde girl, moving a copy of *We Are The New Romantics* so we can both sit down, Jono hands me a glass of champagne and helpfully informs me, by whispering in my ear, that she's 'a complete slut' called Holly.

Opposite the sofa, above what looks like a very expensive sound system, there's a canvas hanging on the wall. *WE ARE GOING TO START A COMMUNE WHEN WE GIVE UP OUR JOBS IN THE CALL CENTRE* is written in large red letters along the bottom.

114

It's 2 a.m. and by now everyone except Patrick is in the living room. Jono and the brunette are standing in front of the sound system, taking a long time to select a new CD, and I'm next to Holly on one of the sofas, watching her apply some red lipstick to Rupert's lips because she thinks he'd look good as a girl. She's giggling while messily outlining his mouth and smearing some of the excess on his cheeks, and he's just smiling and lazily strumming a guitar. We're all drinking champagne.

Just Can't Get Enough by Depeche Mode starts playing at the exact moment Patrick enters the room. He's holding a baggie and an old copy of *Arena* with Mischa Barton on the cover. He comes over to the sofa and moves us out of the way, laying the magazine out flat before getting down on his knees.

'That won't work mate,' says Jono, walking over to the sofa. 'Look, the pages are all curling up . . . '

'Use this,' says Rupert, standing up and handing Patrick a credit card.

'Yeah, that'll work,' says Jono, nodding. I roll my eyes.

'Hey, help yourself,' says Patrick, after doing a line. 'The more the merrier . . . '

He gets up and leaves the room, before returning a moment later on the phone. I try to listen in and think he says 'They need to look young' but I can't really hear what he's saying because Holly is giggling so loudly. She does a line and then the brunette does one too. Jono helps himself to a couple of lines and then I do the next one. The feeling is intense and, after I do a second, I take some of the excess on the tip of my finger, rubbing it into my gums. As I do this, Holly kisses me hard on the mouth.

'Good shit, right?' she says, smiling, before reclining on the sofa in a daze.

115

I'm in one of Rupert's three bedrooms on a futon with Holly and we're both in our underwear and quite drunk and the lights are off and I can't remember lighting the candles but I can still make out her pretty face and it seems like we've been kissing for hours and she has a tongue-piercing and feels good but then she breaks off kissing me and stands up and walks over towards the door.

'Would you like me to dance for you?' she asks in a sweet voice, smiling confidently and already starting to sway.

'OK . . . ' I say, not sure what to expect.

She dances, moving gently, her eyes closed, and runs her hands through her long blonde hair. She's very thin and her breasts are small but firm, and as she takes off her panties I notice her pussy is unshaven, which makes me wonder how young she is and think of the word 'innocence' and how I am taking it from her, right now, in a room belonging to a model I barely know. As I think this, she comes over to the bed and kisses me softly on the mouth, her hand in between my legs.

'What would you like to do to me?' she asks, the smile turning into a mischievous grin. I notice that her tongue-piercing is pink, which makes me think about her age again. 'I have a boyfriend and we've not done it yet, but if you promise to be gentle I'll let you put it in my bum if you want . . . '

Suddenly, there's a knock at the door. It's Rupert. His face is covered in the make-up from earlier and he's only wearing underwear. He looks wired.

'Hey,' I say, poking my head around the door. 'What's up?'

'Alex, you're going to want to see this, um, in the living room,' he says excitedly. I look down and notice he has an erection. 'Don't bother getting dressed, though . . . '

Before I can say anything, he walks away towards the living room. I turn to Holly and ask if she wants to go and see, but she just shrugs and flops back on the futon drunkenly and I realise she's out of it.

I put on my jeans and make my way into the living room. On the sofa in front of me as I enter are two more young girls, neither of whom I recognise. They look Eastern European and are naked on all fours. Jono is sitting between them on the sofa and he's also naked. The girls are kissing him and I notice he has a large erection and he smiles at me when he sees me staring. Rupert is by the window at the back of the room, opposite to where I stand, and is just watching and smiling and he gives me the thumbs up when our eyes meet. To my right, on the other sofa, the brunette is lying naked and she's playing with herself and giggles when I look at her. To my left, Patrick is holding a small camcorder and behind him, on the flat-screen television, is an image of Jono and the two girls naked.

'Alex!' he says, now pointing the camera at me. 'I've booked some . . . *entertainment*. Care to join us?'

Before I can say anything, Holly pushes past me in the doorway.

'Where do you want me?' she says, dancing naked in the centre of the room.

116

I'm standing in men's division looking at the board and I notice that Patrick's card is no longer there and when I look at the boys starting with the letter 'A' I see that my card has changed and now has the *Dazed* cover with Kate Moss as the image and next to my card where Andreas should be there's some boy called Benjamin Z and I look to see if Andreas has moved somehow but I can't see him.

'Sorry about that babes but I just needed to take that call,' says Jo, removing her headset and turning to face me. 'What's up?'

'Um, nothing . . . ' I say, still looking for Andreas. 'I just, um, thought I'd check in and see if there was any, um, news . . . '

I turn around and she looks at her computer, getting me up on her screen. It's blank.

'You're clear hun,' she says flatly, not looking at me.

'Oh yeah, Paul Smith has gone off babes,' says Sam from across the desk. 'Just so you know . . . ' She goes back to her screen.

A pause.

'Um, I thought . . . well, I thought it was looking pretty good . . . ' I say, letting out a hollow laugh.

'Yeah I know babes, but sometimes clients are like that,' says Jo, looking across at Sam who, at that exact moment, looks up at her. 'One minute they love you . . . '

'Alex, options come off all the time,' says Sam, now looking at her screen again. 'You should know that by now.'

'Yeah but I thought, um . . . what about the Steven Klein shoot and, um, New York?'

'That's still on option babes,' says Jo, her back to me. 'Don't worry. These things happen . . . '

117

I leave my agency and call Patrick to see if he knows anything about Andreas.

'Hey Alex,' he says, after only one ring. 'Can I call you back later? I'm kind of in the middle of something. My dad has got me a place at King's for next year and I'm going travelling after Christmas. I know some people in Tokyo, from the modelling days, so I'm going to fly out and see where I end up. I'm just looking at flights now.'

'Um, cool, that sounds really cool . . . ' I say, trailing off. I'm walking along Great Marlborough Street and a black man looks me up and down and stares at me as I pass by, which makes me feel uncomfortable, even vulnerable, rather than flattered.

'Alex, is everything OK?' says Patrick.

'Yeah . . . um, well . . . actually, I wanted to ask you . . . have you heard from Andreas? He's not on the board anymore, at the agency, and . . . ' I trail off again and turn around. The fruity-looking man looks back over his shoulder, making eye contact with me. 'Patrick?' I continue. 'Did you hear me?'

'Um, yeah Alex, sorry I . . . um . . . I thought you knew . . . '

'Knew what?' I ask, by now tired of people thinking I know things that I patently don't. 'I thought Andreas was in Milan but now I'm not so sure . . . '

'He *was* in Milan, Alex,' he interrupts. 'He stayed out there and ran up a huge bill, not going to castings, smoking weed, pissing off his agency and . . . ' He trails off.

'Yeah?' I say, entering the melee of Oxford Circus. I notice that the scouse preacher who's always there has been replaced with another man – less friendly-looking, almost seedy even – who is mumbling into a megaphone and I can't make out what he's saying, what he wants me to do, how I can be saved. 'Patrick?'

'Well, I heard – and this is only a rumour – I heard that he got arrested for trying to buy heroin off an undercover policeman and, um, his parents were supposed to have bailed him out and now, um, I think he's back in Germany . . . but I don't know for sure . . . ' In the underground station a black and white image of me lying shirtless on a yacht in Cannes drinking champagne for the YSL campaign is on a large billboard near the ticket machines and the same image also lines the escalators leading down to the Bakerloo Line southbound platform. I am everywhere. 'Alex, did you hear me?' Patrick continues, his voice fading because my signal is failing. 'Don't worry . . . it's probably . . . just . . . '

118

I'm walking around Notting Hill on my way to the only casting I've had all week but I can't find the right number and I'm starting to think I'm lost. I've walked up and down Portobello Road twice now, past a large group of Italian tourists dressed in matching red scarves and grouped together in the middle of the road, blocking my progress, and I'm pretty sure the address is wrong.

As I pass a mews street for the third time and contemplate calling Jo to check the address, I see a young man playfully holding a baby above his head. I stop, my head poking around the corner, and watch as he holds the baby close to him and walks towards a Range Rover parked in an open garage across the street. When I look closer, as he turns around, I realise it's Hugo.

He's wearing a loose-fitting white shirt with the sleeves casually rolled up and a pair of blue jeans. He's tan, like he's just been away, and he looks really good. I start to walk down the mews street, desperately thinking of the best thing to say to him, but stop as I spot Katie coming out of a house, locking the door behind her.

I stand in a small doorway and am filled with dread as I watch them furtively, and they're laughing and Hugo says something that makes Katie hit him playfully on the shoulder and then she takes the baby in her arms.

I'm close enough to make out the baby's features. I think

it's a boy and he has blonde hair and is handsome. He looks happy.

I watch Katie place the baby in the back seat and then get into the car. As Hugo closes the door behind her and looks up the street, I think he sees me. I step backwards into the doorway so I'm standing upright, back to the door, but when I slowly tilt my head around the doorway to look again I realise he's no longer looking at me.

The car speeds past and I turn to face the doorway, hiding my face. I think to myself, while cowering in the doorway and starting to sweat despite the cold, that Hugo has black hair and Katie is a brunette, which makes me recall the last time I saw him and what he'd said to me.

'Fucking hell, you don't know,' he'd said. 'You really don't know do you?'

'No, clearly I do not fucking know about Katie!' I'd yelled, thinking of the times we were together, and how Hugo couldn't possibly know.

'Alexander, I know, OK?' he'd said, not looking at me and by now on the verge of tears. 'Don't make me say it, Alexander.'

And then I knew he'd somehow found out, and I just stood there, in his apartment, frozen, and tried to deflect it onto him because I thought he'd slept with Nathalie, but I didn't really think that, deep down, because I knew Hugo, and I knew Nathalie, and I knew they would never do that to me.

'We're not together,' he'd said. 'Do you think I'd do that to you? I'm not like you, Alexander.'

'I'm not like you,' he'd said.

But I'd pushed him on it anyway, still wanting him to just come out and say it.

'Look, me and Katie we . . . we were never together or anything . . . it was just once when, um, we were drunk . . . ' I'd said, lying.

And it was then that he'd said something that confused me.

'Well you must be really good then,' he'd said, laughing.

'What do you mean?' I'd said, confused, at the time anyway.

'Are you telling me you only slept together one time?' he'd said, his eyes fixed on mine.

'Yes, Hugo. I promise you, we were only together once, and it was a mistake. I'm sorry, OK? Forgive me, please . . . ' I'd said, lying to his face again.

'It's too late for that, Alexander. And really, you shouldn't be asking *me* to forgive you,' he'd said.

'You shouldn't be asking *me* to forgive you,' he'd said. What did he mean? Why couldn't I ask for his forgiveness? We were meant to be friends weren't we?

'I don't understand . . . ' I'd said.

'Look,' he'd said, 'you don't know what I thought you knew, when you came here, OK? I can't say it. I can't bear to say it and look you in the eye.'

And then he'd grabbed me, his anger spilling over, and shoved me into the lift.

'Talk to Katie,' he'd said, and the doors closed, on me, on us.

We haven't spoken since.

I never did talk to Katie.

And now, the two of them are together, and they have a baby.

The baby looks nothing like Hugo.

I'm not like you.

The baby looks like me.

119

On my way home I pass a Waitrose and remember that I have nothing in and outside I see someone who works in the supermarket moving on an emaciated *Big Issue* seller who's standing in front of the entrance and I decide I need a cigarette so slip into an alleyway and down some steps and as I check my pockets to see if I have any Davidoff Lights left I almost trip over a beggar who's sleeping on a bed made of damp cardboard at the bottom of the steps and I panic and rid myself of any loose change I have by dropping it at his feet and I walk away and then find myself starting to run.

120

I'm with my dad at Claridge's and have ordered the cannon of salt marsh lamb with crystallised walnuts, but I can't stop thinking about Hugo and Katie and the baby so I just keep moving it around the plate.

'You haven't touched your lamb, Alexander,' my dad says. I stare at the food in front of me but don't really see it. 'And do you not like the wine? I thought it was a pretty good vintage . . . '

For some reason my dad has ordered a bottle of the Dominique Laurent 1998 Gevrey-Chambertin, which, if I'm honest, means nothing to me but then again it doesn't really matter because I'm not paying.

'So . . . how have you been?' he asks, urging me to speak, tell him about my feelings – y'know, open up. I look up from my plate and we make eye contact, probably for the first time since we sat down. He looks handsome in a blue Paul Smith suit and crisp white shirt, no tie, his blonde hair neat and tidy from a recent trim.

'I'm fine,' I reply flatly. I take a large gulp of wine but can't taste anything.

'Well I've been trying to get in touch with you for a while now and . . . '

'I know,' I interrupt. 'I got the messages.'

A pause.

'If you got the messages,' he says, frowning, the wrinkles in his tan face becoming more apparent, 'why didn't you let me know you were OK?'

'I've been busy,' I answer dismissively.

I look around the restaurant and think to myself that we should've gone somewhere else, somewhere younger, but my dad had already made reservations and apparently they're hard to get, unless you're staying in the hotel. I didn't tell him I'd booked a room for later.

'How's the modelling going?' he asks, trying again to reach out, play at being a father.

'Do you care?' I reply, under my breath.

'Pardon, I didn't quite catch . . . '

'There are no girls in here,' I interrupt, looking away and around the restaurant again. 'Great choice . . . ' I add, shaking my head and taking another large gulp of wine.

'OK then,' my dad says, clearly exasperated. 'Have it your way.' I glance at him as he removes the napkin from his lap and carefully dabs his mouth, before standing and walking over to me. 'I'm going to the bathroom,' he says in a low voice. Pausing by my side, he seems to consider placing his hand on my shoulder, just for a moment, but then decides against it and walks away.

I feel like people are looking at me and I really want a cigarette but can't or won't get up from the table, and I start to think about earlier when I called Patrick because I wanted to know where he got the call girls from, last time, and I'm beginning to regret making a booking and feel ridiculous but my dad comes back before I can even contemplate doing anything about it.

'Have you spoken to your mother?' he asks as our mains are served, attempting once more to break the silence, to fill the void that exists between us. 'How is she? Is she well?'

'How's Catherine?' I reply in a flash. 'Is *she* well?'

A pause. I stare at him across the table, and eagerly await his response.

'I think we're going to need more wine,' he finally says, looking away and refusing to take the bait. Before I can say anything, a waiter – handsome, probably an out of work model – suddenly appears at our table, and my dad orders another bottle. 'It's funny you should mention her actually, but Catherine told me about your little run in at Shoreditch House,' my dad says, after the waiter disappears. He's smiling, as if this is some kind of private joke.

'Oh yeah?' I say, sitting up slightly. I picture that day, in the changing room, and then those women giggling at the table, Catherine winking at me. I study my dad's face and try to read his mind, but the handsome waiter appears again with the wine, interrupting us momentarily. He takes what feels like a long time to open the bottle, before asking my dad to try it. The waiter keeps glancing at me and, from the knowing expression on his face, I start to think that he's been listening in to our conversation. Moments ago, unsolicited, he suddenly appeared after my dad's comment about needing more wine. He must have been listening in, I think to myself. This realisation makes me even more uncomfortable than I already am, and I avoid eye contact with him as he tops up my glass.

'You think I'm stupid, don't you?' my dad says, leaning forwards. 'You think I'm blind, Alexander. You actually think I don't know . . .'

'What do you mean?' I interrupt, by now agitated and looking around the restaurant, at nothing in particular, just to avoid his gaze.

' . . . that I don't know she sees other men, young men, from time to time,' he continues, almost whispering now. I glance at him and he's still smiling, as if pleased with himself, and I start to consider what he might mean by 'young men', and then whether I even care. 'You actually think I've got to this age and had the success I've had, while all the time not knowing what goes on right under my nose, don't you?' I'm staring at the handsome waiter, standing nearby, and am now convinced he's listening in. 'Do you know why I call you, Alexander?' my dad says, leaning back in his chair. 'Do you know why I bother you and want to see you when I'm in town, even though you resent me for it?'

'No,' I reply, still staring at the waiter. We make eye contact and I look away, back at my dad. 'No I don't. Please tell me . . . '

'It's because, believe it or not, I *do* care about you.'

'It's so quiet in here,' I say, trying to change the subject. I look around again at surrounding tables, and by now am convinced that everyone in the restaurant, not merely the waiter, is following our conversation.

'Despite what you might think, Alexander, I was always faithful to your mother,' my dad says, after a while. 'I mean, until near the end, when it was . . . '

'Hey, man,' I shout to the waiter, cutting off my dad, 'what agency are you with?' I no longer care about the surrounding tables. In fact, I want people to hear me.

'What do you mean?' he replies, coming over to our table.

'You're not a model?' I say, frowning to convey faux-incredulity, as if to flatter him.

'Um, no . . . '

'You should look into it. I'm with Creative. You should

171

check them out. Ask for Jo. Tell her I sent you.'

'Alexander,' my dad says pleadingly, leaning forwards in his chair so he's only inches away from me. The waiter edges away from the table, but not so far as to be unable to continue following our confrontation. 'Alexander, I just . . . ' my dad continues, his voice lower now, 'I just didn't want to spend the rest of my life with someone I . . . '

'Why are you telling me this?' I interrupt. We make eye contact, briefly, and in that moment I think of that evening, just before I went off to university, when my parents told me they were separating. They tried to laugh it off and even joke about it, to reassure me, I guess. While they were telling me that everything was going to be OK, that nothing was going to change, that they both still loved me, I just stared at the television. The news was on, but at some point the volume had been turned down.

'I talked to Nathalie's dad last week,' he says, after a moment. 'I know about you two. That's a shame . . . '

'Yeah?' I say, leaning back in my chair so we're no longer face to face. 'And why's that?'

'Because you love her,' he says, staring back at me. 'Or am I wrong about that too?' I sip my wine while focusing on the waiter who is still standing nearby, still clearly listening in. 'Don't you want to be happy, Alexander?' my dad says, after another moment. I look at him across the table and he looks back, as if he's looking beyond me, even into me, and smiles. I look away, at the waiter again, and think to myself that I've seen him at castings, and that when he said he wasn't a model perhaps he was joking or being ironic or whatever. 'Why do you want to blame everyone else for your life?' my dad continues, reaching across the table and placing his hand on mine. 'I know you don't want to hear this, especially from me, but if I could give you one piece of advice, it would be to look at yourself – look beyond what you see in the mirror, on the surface – and take responsibility for your own happiness.' We hold eye contact again across the table, but I've stopped listening and am no longer even seeing him. Instead, an image of Nathalie, the last time I saw her, flashes in front of my eyes. She's walking away, back towards the villa, and I don't stop her. My hand reaches out but she suddenly moves even farther into the distance. 'This world is a very lonely place,' my dad is saying, 'if you don't have someone to share it with . . . '

And in that moment, as I try to block out my dad, this conversation, the handsome waiter, I realise something. It's me, in the image, moving backwards, farther away from her.

'I have to be somewhere,' I say, pulling my hand away swiftly and standing abruptly to leave.

'Alexander . . . ' my dad calls out, but it's too late.

It's too late because I've already turned my back on him, alone at the table, and am now walking away.

121

I'm lying on a King-size bed in my room, thinking of Nathalie, staring at my phone and wondering whether I should cancel the girl. This goes on for maybe half an hour until there's a knock at the door, and I realise it's too late.

I open the door and a tall blonde girl is standing there. She's not what I expected. She's young, maybe early twenties, wearing a white blouse, a black pencil skirt and high heels, as if she's come from a well-paid office job. She smiles and I move to the side, inviting her to enter.

The girl's working name is Chelsea. I chose her because I support the football team and because she has incredible tits. Patrick gave me a website, rather than a phone number, and said I should check out the profiles of the girls, their photos and location, and also carefully read the user reviews, as it were, before making a booking.

'Um, I have the money for you,' I say, walking over to the bed and taking £1,000 from my Vivienne Westwood jacket pocket. I'd asked if I could pay cash and they'd said I could, as long as it was upfront, so before meeting my dad I withdrew the remainder of my YSL money. This will be enough for the whole night.

'Do you want, um, something to drink?' I ask, for some reason nervous. The girl hasn't said anything yet and only smiles when I hand her the money. 'Um, there's the mini-bar or . . . um . . . room service . . . '

'I'm OK, thank you,' she says. She's well-spoken and her accent, what little she has of one, is hard to place. Probably a university student, I think to myself.

'You don't mind if I have a drink, do you?' I ask.

'No,' she says, looking bored.

'It would make me, um, more comfortable, I think, if you had a drink with me . . . not much, if that's not allowed . . . only one . . . ' She just stands there, shifts her feet and looks uncomfortable. 'Um, y'know, I'm more Richard Gere than Jack the Ripper so don't worry,' I continue, trying to smile in a non-creepy way. I expected her to say she doesn't usually get calls from models but that's probably not true and, well, why would she say that anyway? 'I've never done this before . . . um . . . I bet you hear that a lot!' I say, laughing nervously. 'Sorry, I'm such an idiot. Take pity on me, please.' I smile. 'I just want to relax . . . '

'OK,' she says, smiling back, 'but I can only have one . . . '

122

Early the next morning, while it's still dark outside, I wake up and realise the girl is gone. On the pillow next to me, there's a note: *You are very sweet. See you again some time . . . ?* *Chelsea* x

123

Later that afternoon, I head over to Nathalie's work. I've never been one for grand gestures but I think if I just turn up, show my face, I might somehow be able to convince her to talk to me.

Nathalie works in a trendy, glass-fronted office building in the heart of Noho, just off Charlotte Street. There's table top Pacman in reception and they give you smoothies or large glass bottles of mineral water from huge refrigerators if you're meeting someone. I don't have an appointment, though, so I just wait, slumped on a bean bag, while a middle-aged and rather officious receptionist calls to find out if Nathalie's at her desk.

'Sir,' she says after a moment, 'I'm sorry to have to tell you that the lady in question is away from her desk. Can I ask what it is concerning?'

No you fucking can't, you nosy cow, I think to myself.

'Um, no, that won't be necessary,' I say. 'It was, um, nothing important . . . '

'Sir,' she pipes up again as I walk over to the door, 'would you like me to take a message?'

I consider this for a moment. Would Nathalie speak to me again, take everything back, simply because I visited her at her office? After everything, would a flying visit make any difference at all? And if she asks, do I even know why I'm here?

I dump the flowers on top of an overflowing rubbish bin on the pavement outside. As I make my way back to the underground station, I pass a billboard with an ad for Nicotinel and it says *Willpower Required* in the small print and I start to feel really cold.

I look up at the sky and notice it's almost dark, and it seems the days are growing shorter and shorter.

124

I haven't had any castings all week but when I mention it to Jo she just says 'There's not much going on right now y'know it's very quiet' and I say 'But isn't there anything?' and she says 'I have a couple of go-sees for you tomorrow one with Leo who's doing editorials for *FHM* and *Maxim* . . . ' and then Sam interrupts and says 'I was at a party with Kate Moss and she's not working and if Kate Moss isn't working nobody's working!' and she laughs hysterically and Jo laughs too.

125

I'm in the underground station, topping up my oyster card before making my way over to Woolwich Arsenal for my first go-see, but I'm daydreaming in the queue and a girl behind me says 'It's your turn' and then 'Excuse me you're next' but I don't realise she's talking to me and as I turn to smile, apologise, I see Frankie joining the queue behind her and before I can do anything we make eye contact and it's too late.

'Um . . . hi,' I say, trying to smile.

'Hi,' she says in a soft voice. 'How are you babes? You look really good.'

'Fucking hell some of us need to be somewhere . . . ' mumbles the girl as she pushes past me to the ticket machine.

I move closer to Frankie and stand with her in the queue. On the wall to my left, there's a small sticker with the words *Capitalism Is Bad Don't Vote* in the middle of a billboard advertising the elections.

'So, what are you up to nowadays?' she says, staring straight ahead and not at me. 'I saw the YSL campaign. You looked really handsome.'

'Um, thanks . . . ' I reply. 'It's, um, pretty quiet right now but, um, I've been doing OK, considering . . . '

'Are you seeing anyone right now?' she says, suddenly looking at me. In that moment, I think of Paris, of Bailey, and I want to say something, anything, to change the subject, but instead I just smile. 'Is that a "no"?' she says, moving closer to me and placing her hand on my arm.

'Um, well . . . I'm not, um . . . '

'It's a simple question, Alex,' she says, laughing. 'Do you want to know if I'm seeing someone?' She's stroking my arm now.

'Aren't you seeing Bailey?' I say, immediately regretting it.

'Is that what he told you?' she says, turning away and then smiling. She walks over to the ticket machine and I follow.

'Maybe. Why? Is it true?' I say, leaning over her as she touches her Oyster card against the reader.

'Oh, I already have credit!' she says, letting out a small laugh. I step towards the ticket machine and top up my oyster card, and Frankie stays by my side. 'Alex . . . ' she says, suddenly positioning herself in between the machine and me, biting her lip. 'Do you want to come to a party tonight . . . with me?'

As she says this, I think of something Nathalie once wrote as part of a poetry module she was taking, in our final year, after she'd found out that I'd slept with Katie.

These broken stories of mine, told only because I yearn to feel,
Those broken promises of yours, which only made me learn to kneel.

126

My second go-see is all the way back across town miles from the nearest tube on an industrial estate in Ealing and after walking for ten maybe fifteen minutes I see a boy coming towards me on a busy main road and he looks like Tobias but when I get closer I realise it's not Tobias and he gives me directions which help a little but after spending what feels like a long time looking for the entrance and being told by a rude bloke through a speaker 'Go back to where you came in turn right there's only one right mate' I spend a minute max in the place trying on a jacket that doesn't fit for a photographer whose name is Bam I think and he's aloof and utterly indifferent and I feel like I've been here before.

127

By the time I leave, it's gone 5 p.m. and is already dark. I make my way back to the station and it's cold and I pull my Alexander McQueen trench coat around me tightly, wrapping myself in it as if it's a blanket.

Crossing the busy main road, I start to think about whether I should go to that party with Frankie tonight, whether it would be a mistake.

As I pass what looks like a bank, I notice it's closed and see a beggar lying in the doorway, in front of a large window that has an ornate Christmas tree display in it, and he's trying to get warm in a torn and filthy sleeping bag.

128

I'm with Frankie at the party in Kentish Town and it's in an enormous Victorian town house and on arrival we're both assured by the person throwing the party who's a rich boy called Fionn that we can trash it as much as we like because the house is getting refurbished soon.

For some reason everything is purple in the house purple floors purple walls purple furniture and the theme is mods and rockers I think but neither of us has dressed up and I'm already pretty drunk when I arrive but after I'm handed a plastic cup of purple punch that keeps getting refilled every time I enter a new room and given that this house is huge and has a lot of rooms I'm really drunk and the party soon gets going.

Frankie and I are on a purple mattress on the second floor and we're next to a weird-looking girl with a lip-piercing and every time I open my eyes while kissing Frankie she's looking at me but isn't smiling and actually looks upset maybe even jealous and I think I recognise her but I know deep down that I don't.

I've had so much to drink by around 3 a.m. that I can't be sure of what's happening because everyone is dressed like it's the 80s and purple is everywhere and loud music is playing throughout the house and it sounds like *Mirror in the Bathroom* by The English Beat which doesn't seem appropriate to me and at one point feeling really drunk I say 'Why do I do drugs?' not to anyone in particular and Frankie says 'Boredom' and just smiles seductively and kisses me hard on the mouth.

129

The next morning, on my way home, I decide to go via my agency to check in. It's cold and I'm wearing Frankie's John Galliano ski hat because she says it suits me.

When I arrive, Jo and Sam are both on the phone and I have to wait in reception because everyone's too busy in the agency to let models just hang around. I mumble 'That's a first' to myself while reading an old copy of *Numero* and wondering what happened to *that* shoot, but I don't bother complaining.

I decide I need a drink so I go to the kitchen and help myself to some fresh orange juice from the fridge. After finishing the entire carton, I wander into a small room with only cushions for furniture that Sam likes to call 'the snug' to wait for Jo.

'What's with the hat?' she says as she enters and sits down on a huge cushion next to me.

'I'm very well, thanks,' I say sarcastically. 'Thanks for asking . . . '

'Babes . . . ' she says, tilting her head disapprovingly. 'Don't start. We're up to our necks right now and . . . '

'I thought it was quiet?' I say, interrupting her.

A pause.

'OK, so I'm glad you've come in because I need to talk to you,' she says, getting up and closing the door.

'Oh yeah? Sounds ominous . . . ' I say, laughing.

'We've got bad news,' she says, sitting down again and pulling a ridiculous face like she's about to say 'Eek!' while placing her hand on my thigh.

'OK . . . '

'Steven Klein is not going to happen.'

Another pause.

'Um . . . why?' I manage.

'It's simple. We sent Polaroids of you to them last week because they wanted to see your body and, well, they got back to us yesterday and said they were looking for someone bigger.'

'Um, I don't understand . . . ' I say, after a moment.

'They think you need to put on more weight. Look, it's come up before. Paul Smith went off because they wanted someone with more bulk.' She touches my stomach at this point, which causes me to flinch. 'The skinny look isn't in right now . . . '

'Hang on,' I say, sounding hurt. 'I'm skinny all of a sudden? This has never come up before . . . '

'I know but that's because, well, we thought you were the right look. Hey, you did so well in Paris and Milan but the shows are, well, different. It's not uncommon for fragrance ads to go to guys with a bigger physique anyway, but muscles are definitely back in. Just look at Chad White . . . '

'Who the fuck is Chad White?' I say, interrupting.

'Look Alex, Sam and I have been talking to Guy and he agrees with us and thinks you could be huge if you put on weight, so we're going to get you down to the gym more often to work with a trainer, and see what happens. It's pretty quiet over Christmas anyway . . . '

'Do you know who they went for?' I say, cutting her off. 'I mean, instead of me . . . '

'I'm not sure, babes,' she says. 'Some Canadian boy . . . '

'Bailey?' I interrupt again, staring at her. 'Is his name Bailey?'

'I have no idea,' she says, looking puzzled. 'Why?'

'Doesn't matter,' I say, looking away. 'So, um, what about New York?' I ask, after a moment.

'It was your agency there that first said you needed more weight,' she says, her expression earnest. 'We won't send you out there until you look the way they want you to look.'

'OK . . . ' I say, looking away again. I think of the full name of my agency, the words 'Model Management', and then I think of Patrick and the girl with freckles, and an image of Andreas the last time I saw him flashes in front of my eyes. 'So, um, can I leave now?' I ask, already standing.

'Sure,' she says, standing and then opening the door. 'Look, babes,' she adds as I pass her in the doorway, 'Brad Pitt was told to put on weight early in his career and, hey, look at him now . . . '

130

On my way back to Oxford Circus, I see a young beggar holding a *Big Issue* and he says 'Spare some change?' and then smiles when I look at him. We hold eye contact as I approach the opening to the underground station, and I notice his teeth are rotten.

As I pass by, I almost smile at him but instead look down at my feet.

131

I've just left a casting for Topman and I felt really old and that maybe I shouldn't be there and dazed and borderline dehydrated I walk down Oxford Street towards Selfridges because I need to return some DSquared jeans I spent way too much money on and as I listen to *Mr. Bojangles* on my iPhone I see an ad for 'luxury' mineral water in a diamante-encrusted bottle and think to myself that if ads sell the idea of clean pure water now then why not one day air?

I wonder to myself whether this is an innovative idea as I wander into Selfridges past maybe a dozen mannequins that all have paper bags with an outline of a generic female face on the heads and on the first floor after walking past two empty checkout desks I eventually track down a man who looks like he can help me and he's short maybe 5' 7" and tan with a low cut V-neck T-shirt and a very hairy chest and he's moody and definitely not impressed when I tell him I want to return the jeans but when we walk past the YSL stand to the checkout there's a large poster of the campaign and it's a black and white image of me lying shirtless on a yacht in Cannes drinking champagne and I think he realises who I am because he smiles at me as I walk away.

On my way out of Selfridges I'm still thirsty and as I make my way through the crowds I cross over and walk down South Molton Street and there's a beggar sitting on the pavement and he's not wearing any shoes or socks and he's holding a traffic cone to his mouth and even though I have my headphones in I can still hear him singing so I remove my right headphone to listen and when I put it back in as I pass by I suddenly notice that the song I'm listening to is *Hear My Song* by Louie Austen and this makes me turn around but when I do I see that the beggar is no longer there and the cone is upright and people are just walking by and carrying on as normal.

I slip down an alleyway into a small courtyard that feels almost serene compared to where I've just been and then I stop in front of a restaurant that looks closed.

I notice it's starting to rain, and everything slows down.

I light a cigarette, gather my thoughts, and look at my reflection in the window of the restaurant. The glass shows up the contours of my face, the contrast where my cheekbones protrude, and I look tired, perhaps even more so than usual. As I take another drag, I adjust my perspective and through the glass see a couple talking to one another across a small table, which surprises me as the restaurant appeared empty at first glance.

I look closer and can see the back of a girl's head. She has blonde, boyish hair, but I can't see her face. Over her shoulder, I can see a handsome man – not a model, but good-looking nonetheless – and he's talking and waving his hands, like he's telling a joke. Even though I can only see the back of the girl's head, I can tell she's enjoying every minute of the story. They look happy.

After a moment, the man reaches across the table and touches her hand. He says something with an earnest expression on his face and then smiles before standing, walking over to the girl and kissing her softly on the lips.

As he walks away towards the back of the restaurant, talking to the manager like they're old friends, I look back at the girl, who has turned slightly so I can now see her profile. I recognise her instantly as she rubs the back of her head to give her hair more volume, a gesture that I am so very familiar with, that we used to laugh about, and she smiles to herself, almost self-consciously, as if she knows she's being watched.

'You know what your problem is, Alex?' she'd said, backing away from me and no longer crying. 'You don't know how to love.'

132

I'm dreaming.

I'm in a bar, alone.

It's late.

I'm drinking a purple cocktail in an ornate Martini glass, like the ones in Buddha Bar in Paris.

'This is really good, thanks,' I say to the barman, who looks like a model.

'You're welcome,' he replies, nodding.

On a table behind me, a middle-aged man who looks like a pimp is obnoxiously groping a woman.

She's a prostitute.

Both are clearly drunk.

I can't avoid staring at him, watching his every move with sneering disgust.

As he finishes his drink, he orders a waiter to call him a cab. The waiter, dressed in a black shirt, black tie and garish purple waistcoat, politely tells him that he can't, that he doesn't have a phone number, but that cabs drive by the entrance all night. The drunk shouts at the waiter and tells him to go outside and hail a cab. The waiter, clearly embarrassed, apologises and escapes to find a manager.

As they leave, I finish my drink, nod to the waiter and follow them outside.

'Good-night,' the waiter says. 'See you again soon . . . '

The woman staggers off while the man walks in the direction of the river.

I follow him along Waterloo Bridge.

'Hey, wait up sir!' I shout. 'I think you left something behind in the bar.'

'What?' he snarls, looking over his shoulder.

'Here, slow down, I have something for you.'

He starts to quicken and reaching the other side descends the steps to the South Bank but I easily catch up to him and put my hand on his shoulder and he yells 'You fucking faggot!' and swings wildly at me but misses and then I stab him with a large knife that actually looks like a sword in fact it is a sword and I push him down the rest of the steps and then wipe the sword on the front of my jeans but the sword is somehow clean already.

Above his body is some stencil graffiti of a prostitute.

She Walks In Beauty Like The Night is written above her head in large purple letters.

Scrawled in black marker, defacing the portrait, there's a speech bubble from her mouth.

It reads: *Fuck Off Banksy*.

133

My world is one that is not yet fully realised, one that holds within it so much potential. But this is the nauseating truth of a world in which anything is possible. Nothing is also possible.

I'm wasting the day in a Starbucks off Piccadilly, staring aimlessly, from my window seat, at the flower stall on the other side of the street. It's bitterly cold outside but the sun is shining and Frank Sinatra is playing and, as the blurred images of people's lives and troubles pass by, something is growing, deep inside. I'm moved to tears.

This town, is a lo-sin' town . . .

It's a mis-erable town . . .

It's a no-where town . . .

And yet, as the song starts to fade, so too does the sensation.

And, I am leavin' this town . . .

You better believe, that I'm leavin' this town . . .

I stare at my reflection in the window, an image that rests, as if indecisive, between the real and the unreal, indefinite and without true form, but also a version of me, of my existence here in this place.

We are not really here.

As my perspective begins to change, I focus on a solitary figure across the street: a young beggar, rummaging through a rubbish bin while people pass by ignoring him or simply not noticing him at all.

I watch as he picks out a magazine and holds it in his right hand while digging deeper with the left, and I think I recognise the face on the magazine cover but I can't be sure.

He looks up and across the road and, in that moment, we make eye contact and I recognise him and there's a connection and it feels like something unbreakable between us.

As he smiles, I look at his rotten teeth.

I stare at him, wondering just how young he is.

I'm not like you.

We will win.

You don't know how to love.

We will win.

We will win.